CW01455755

For All the Times I Tried to Say Goodbye

Lorenzo di Bernardo

For All the Times I Tried to Say Goodbye
© 2025 Lorenzo di Bernardo
All rights reserved.

ISBN: 9798286931477 | ASIN: B0FC5N7YVY
Imprint: Independently published
Third Edition, 2025

Cover design by Lorenzo di Bernardo
Edited by Lorenzo di Bernardo
Published by Lorenzo di Bernardo

For permissions and inquiries, contact:
forallthetimesbook@gmail.com

To resilience.
Without the ache, this story would have
never found its voice.

"The past is never dead. It's not even past."
William Faulkner

Contents

1.

SILENCE

"We are healed of a suffering only by experiencing it to the full." —Marcel Proust

The sand stretched ahead like an endless, bleached cathedral floor, bronze, and damp with morning dew, wind-carved into delicate whorls. Each step sent up a haze of dust, as though even the very act of moving left a faint sigh in its wake. The tide had retreated hours ago, peeling back in jagged sheets that cracked under the sun's pallid glare, as if the sea itself had scrubbed the world clean of every vestige of passage. In a few more hours, the water would return in slow, insistent currents—patient arms washing away footprints, hollowing out the hollows of yesterday, erasing the stories embedded in the sand. Ben inhaled deeply, tasting the faint, briny tang of seaweed and salt on the breeze, but his thoughts lay elsewhere—adrift on the frothy crest of his own impermanent world. He began to walk again, boots sinking lightly into the parched grains, eyes narrowed against the diffuse light of a sky strained thin, searching the familiar curve of coastline as though seeking some lost fragment of himself, though he scarcely knew what he hoped to find.

Across the narrow ribbon of coastal road, a sunlit courtyard teemed with the restless hum of careless energy. Umbrellas striped in bruised reds and faded yellows offered scant solace from the glare; beneath them, patrons clung to half-empty glasses, the ice melting in the heat, water beading on cold glass like tear-drops. Laughter ricocheted off ivy-clad walls, mingling with the low murmur of conversation, the rattle of chairs, the scrape of a coffee cup against a saucer. To Ben, it all sounded like a cacophony: harsh, intrusive, as jarring as gull calls overhead. He paused at the edge of the road, his gaze drifting past the court-yard to the pub that dominated one corner of the square. It stood proud on fluted stone pillars; its great doors carved with decorative flourishes promising grandeur. But those heavy portals opened only onto another street, bustling with traffic and neon signs, while the pub's true entrance—a plain glass wall hidden around the back by the bus station—might as well have been invisible. That seamless pane reflected nothing but the dull façades of adjacent shops and sent no invitation to anyone curious enough to seek its interior.

Ben resisted the siren lure of distraction. He turned back to the open water and exhaled, a pale cloud forming briefly around his mouth before dissolving into the cool air. The breeze cut through his jacket pockets, carrying whiffs of kelp and driftwood tangled in the shallows, but none of it reached the coldness that had taken root in his chest. He found the world's relentless pursuit of distraction bewildering: neon signs flickering insipid invitations to spend more, crowds huddled around the comfort of cheap laughter, the clink of glasses masquerading as genuine connection. To him, people drifted past one another like ethereal phantoms, each clutching a fresh joke or another drink as though it might fill the empty cavities inside—a currency he knew all too well couldn't buy relief.

His boots followed the tide line. Solitary. Soundless. Then, unexpectedly, two children's shrill voices pierced the hush. From atop a low stone wall lining the promenade, they leaned forward in playful conspiracy, shrieking and beckoning to a lone boy who lingered near the water's edge. Ben watched, rooted to the spot, as the pair gestured insistently—their calls slicing through his reverie like bright knives. He recognized himself in the solitary figure: once, he had been that boy, abandoned at the margin of childhood's rough games, ribs out-lined by threadbare clothes, shoulders rounded under the weight of scorn. He felt the old sting of humiliation flare in his gut, fol-lowed by a mordant satisfaction: now he was the watcher, no longer the watched.

A brief tableau unfolded before him. A chubby boy, too big for his years, shifted awkwardly in a t-shirt stretched tight across his chest, his cheeks flushed with sun and embarrassment. Next to him, a thin girl with hawk-sharp eyes played the role of director, issuing silent com-mands and jerking her head toward the water. The boy's pleading glances went unanswered; the girl dismissed him with a flick of her hand, then turned away to scheme anew with her companion. Approval—that elusive, glowing prize—hung just out of reach, and the boy sank lower under its absence, shoulders drooping as each ignored request chipped away at his resolve. In that instant, Ben remembered the ache he had carried for so long—a craving for acceptance that had never truly eased, the longing to be included only to be spat back out by biting laughter and cold shoulders. He saw it now for what it was: a feeble currency traded in half-spoken insults, sly glances, and whispered jeers.

He shook his head and forced his legs to move again, stepping past the children's game and receding shadows. In his ears, the soft roar of the returning tide rose like a hymn to something vast and indifferent.

Behind him, joggers threaded along the cracked promenade, faces red, limbs pumped with effort, breath rattling in their lungs like loose stones. They ran endless loops, chasing vague notions of health or happiness, panting after an abstract ideal he considered pathetic. Even the savviest financier, he thought bitterly, would scoff at such a meagre return on

sweat and strained joints. Better—far better—
to starve, at least hunger bore an honest ache,
one he could measure and endure. Yet no matter how many meals he skipped, the ghost of
his overweight childhood-self remained
lodged beneath his skin, waiting to drag him
back into shame with memories of derisive
snorts and pointed fingers.

At last, he came to rest at the water's edge. The
tide sighed out and back, like an exhausted animal. The waves answered no one's pleas,
bowed to no one's approval, and left no trace
of longing behind when they receded. If only
he could surrender so completely—unyielding,
unattached, unburdened by memory. But he
was neither wave nor sand. He was bound to a
body and a mind that conspired to remind him
of every past humiliation, a prisoner of his
own recollections.
He turned away from the sea and skirted back
toward town, passing row upon row of mirrored storefronts, each one a carbon copy of
the last. The shuttered bookstore loomed at
the corner, its dusty windows boarded against
the Sunday quiet, and he felt the weight of
endless, pointless hours pressing down on

him. Sundays here were grey oases of solitude—no crowds, no noise, no distractions to keep the mind from replaying its doubts. Impulsively, he opened the door to the corner café. A tiny bell jingled overhead, its bright tinkle announcing his arrival into an atmosphere of warm air thick with the scent of espresso and the faint sweetness of stale pastries. At a back counter, a young barista with tired eyes delivered the news that closing time would soon be upon them, her voice too bright for so late an hour, as though she clung to hope where none existed. Ben slid onto the stool nearest the door, where a thin draft whispered promises of movement, of agency. He barely glanced at the chalkboard menu scrawled with latte specials and overpriced muffins; instead, he ordered a single shot of black espresso. When it arrived, dark as night in a small cup, he downed it in one sip. The acrid liquid clawed at his throat, igniting a brief warmth in his chest, but it left his heart untouched.

Outside, twilight deepened, and cooler air slithered in on invisible currents. Shop gates began their metallic sighs as they clanged shut, and the first streetlights flickered on, their yellow glow washing over the empty sidewalks. The town seemed to contract around him under the weight of its own insignificance; walls edged closer, ceilings felt lower. Nothing here mattered—except one small creature. Romeo, his tuxedo cat, would be waiting at home, tail flicking like a metronome of welcome.

He rose from the stool, shouldered his jacket, and walked back across the empty square. The rusted hinges of his apartment block door protested as he pushed inside, and the corridor fell silent save for the resound of his footsteps. At home, Romeo met him at the threshold, soft fur brushing against rough denim. The cat's purr vibrated through Ben's leg as he stepped inside, then, satisfied, Romeo slipped away into the shadows of a forgotten corner. Ben closed the door behind him and exhaled, inhaling the muted comfort of wood polish, old carpets, and quiet.

But peace here was always provisional, a surface tension that threatened to break at the slightest disturbance. He crossed the living room, where the dim glow of a single lamp cast elongated shadows across dark wood panelling and a low coffee table strewn with yesterday's mail and an empty whiskey glass. By the doormat lay a small white card, its corners crisp, the surface unblemished even under scrutiny. He stooped to pick it up, his fingertips brushing the weighty embossing:

Dr. Thomas Davenport,
Counselling Psychologist

The card felt unnaturally heavy between his fingers, as though charged with a promise he wasn't sure he wanted to fulfil. He held it still, torn between the urge to crush it in his palm and a subtler pull urging him to keep it safe. Therapy had always struck him as a farce— people paid to listen, offering polite nods in return for personal secrets. And yet the pall of sadness settling over him felt more final than any broken vow he'd ever known.

Before he realized what he was doing, he found himself by the phone, dialling the number printed at the bottom of the card. The cold plastic receiver pressed to his ear as he waited, each ring amplifying his racing pulse. Finally, a calm voice answered: "Hayfield Health

Centre. How may I help you?" Ben's reply came in a hoarse whisper: "Um—hello. I'm calling about... Dr. Davenport." The reception- ist responded with smooth efficiency, her words like a steady hand on a sail: "Would you like to book a session?" His heart thundered in his chest. Closing his eyes, he drew in a long, steadying breath. "Yes," he said, voice firmer now. "I'd like to book an appointment."

Later that evening, he sat alone in his living room, the lamp's amber glow pooling over a battered leather armchair and the teak coffee table. In the kitchen, an old kettle hissed and sputtered on the stove, copper tones dancing in the low light. Ben poured hot water over a tea bag in a chipped enamel mug, steam curl- ing upward in soft, translucent ribbons as its bitter aroma filled the cramped space. He cra- dled the mug between both hands, letting its warmth seep into his knuckles even as his mind churned with anxious anticipation. For a fraction of a moment, he allowed himself to believe that nothing had changed: the cat asleep in the next room, the whine of the ket- tle gone silent, the motionless card on the ta- ble. But beneath that fragile veneer, something had already begun to shift.

The card remained on the table beside him— white, impossible to ignore, its raised letters a quiet beacon. The appointment loomed ahead, a pale point of light in an otherwise dim landscape. It promised something he could not yet name, but for the first time in a long while, he felt lonely enough to hope.

And that, he admitted in a whisper to the shadows, might be enough.

~

The health centre hit Ben with the force of a battering ram against his ribs. Walls of blinding white rose high on either side of him, their surfaces so clinical they might have been scraped from some antiseptic dream. Above, brutal fluorescent bulbs snapped on in relentless chorus, their harsh hum searing the silence as if each flicker were a hammer strike.

19

The tiles underfoot gleamed with such immaculate precision that they seemed to mock him, reflecting the overhead glare in mirrored shards of light. With every footstep his polished boots sounded like cannon fire in an empty hall—an echoing reminder of how alone he felt in this place designed for repair. He'd known it would be oppressive, but nothing had prepared him for the sensation of wandering a cage built to emphasize his absolute foreignness.

His stomach clenched and unclenched like a fist as he navigated the space. He straightened his shoulders, forced his jaw to unclench, rehearsing a calm he didn't feel. Inside, his heart thundered—a private drumroll of panic. At the reception desk a pale woman sat behind a dull computer monitor, her face cast in cold, bluish half-light. She scarcely glanced up as he approached, as though she'd locked his name and date of birth into the machine's consciousness and had no need for further human acknowledgment.

"First floor, room 2," the receptionist murmured, still staring into the blur of the screen. He offered a silent nod, his pulse spiking, and turned toward the narrow metal staircase. Each step groaned under his weight, the railing beside him cold as ice, biting into his palm. Up ahead, the first floor corridor yawned like the throat of some great beast. Doors identical in their bland anonymity stood lined on either side.

 Room 2 lay a dozen steps away but felt an eternity distant. His hand hovered hesitant over the door handle before he drew a trembling breath and rapped his knuckles once against the frame.

When the door swung open, Dr. Davenport emerged from the dim interior like a shadow crystallized in a razor-sharp silhouette. He was tall and lean, every inch the epitome of calculated elegance. However, when he looked at Ben, something flickered brief, uncertain. As if the man behind the doctor had momentarily stepped forward. His attire was immaculate, calculated down to the millimetre. There was something predatory in the grace of his entrance, each step deliberate, each movement choreographed. But it was his eyes—hazel, cool, and focused—that unsettled Ben most. They didn't just look *at* him. They read him.

"Ben." The greeting dropped from Davenport's lips in a low rumble—smooth, velvety, yet freighted with unspoken authority. The sound coiled around Ben's spine, tightening before he even realized it, as if echoing the familiar sound of a long-lost connection.

Ben nodded, his voice trapped somewhere between throat and memory. He stepped into the room, hit instantly by the scent of bleach mingled with something faintly metallic—like secrets rinsed clean but still clinging in the corners. There was a single window, its glass so bright it felt like being stared at by the sun itself. A small desk, two chairs: spare furnishings arranged with the efficiency of an interrogation chamber rather than a sanctuary. Davenport gestured toward the chair opposite him, and Ben sat, shoulders tensing as the doctor's gaze returned—steady, unblinking, absolutely unwavering.

Ben arrived at the studio searching for something he could no longer define. He felt desensitized to the gradual passing of time, his memories like fragile leaves scattered on an abandoned path. Within him lingered a faint memory of when he felt complete, before the burden of unspoken betrayals and buried regrets thickened the air around him. The studio seemed bare, the air crisp with the smell of antiseptic, a place where even silence felt analysed and categorized.

He sensed the doctor's gaze on him—a probing presence that delved into the quiet corners of his mind, compelling him to face his disconnection. That gaze seemed to quietly strip away his pretences, making Ben feel as if the walls were closing in.

He came here to rediscover the missing pieces of himself, to face the quiet pain settled in his chest. But now, he felt exposed, revealed under a light he had long avoided. His past loomed like a dim corridor, each unexamined corner reminding him of the years spent pretending that the absence of something vital was just the natural wear of time.

Yet as he sat there, he sensed the slow, suffocating fog of isolation, how it had enveloped him, piece by piece, until he could no longer see the outline of his own shadow.

Each question Davenport posed was soft—voiced, measured—but carried the iron weight of inevitability. It was as if the man already knew the answers of a conversation that had been playing in his ears ever so relentlessly. Nods, pauses, gentle encouragements: each one felt like a fine-toothed comb raking through his thoughts until every hidden tremor of truth lay bare. He asked about the day Ben stood alone behind the climbing frame, eyes full of gravel and silence. That memory broke something open. Ben couldn't be sure if the warmth in Davenport's gaze was for him, or simply a flare of recognition at someone who didn't expect him to be perfect. Either way, it steadied him more than he liked to admit.

By the session's close, Ben's tense shoulders collapsed. He had surrendered fragments of himself he'd hoarded for years, and in return, he'd found something startling: a perverse, yet known, relief in this meticulous attentiveness.

Later, back in his apartment, Ben lay on the bed, staring at the cracked ceiling, shadows pooling in the corners like secrets left to fester. He had just turned twenty that winter, though the youth of his skin was betrayed by the darkness in his eyes—eyes that had grown up too fast. Like the flat, with boxes left unopened since he moved in a couple of years ago, his mind was cluttered with fractured memories, half-formed and quietly rotting—the sharp lines of Davenport's jaw, the way his lips curved in a smile that was almost cruel, and those eyes, sharp as glass shards, cutting through the fog of Ben's self-doubt. He recalled the doctor's gaze—a quiet force that seemed to peel back the layers of his mind, revealing the raw, untended wounds beneath. It had felt like being stripped bare, but there was something else, too—a chill that clung to his skin, making him shiver long after he had left the studio.

He had not felt this pull in years, the kind that made his pulse beat against his ribs like a trapped animal. Ben had tried, of course. Fleeting girlfriends had come and gone, they had been temporary distractions, their warmth never quite reaching the cold, hollow place inside him. He had told himself it was because he was too damaged, too fragmented by years of isolation and disappointment. He had watched his friends find connections, live lives, and he had tried to follow their paths—Sunday brunches, long drives, shared holidays—but the spark never caught. His interest waned faster than he cared to admit, every touch feeling like an obligation, every kiss an empty task. He had begun to believe that something fundamental within him had broken, that he was perhaps incapable of the connection others took for granted. It had made him question his worth, gnawing at his self-esteem until he could no longer tell if he was lonely by nature or by choice.

Maybe that was why he had leapt at the chance to sit in front of Davenport, to be dissected by that keen mind, hoping that perhaps this man could find the flaw, the crack that had let all his warmth seep out. Davenport, with his rugged handsomeness, had the kind of presence that felt immovable, like a mountain Ben had always longed to lean against. There was stability in the way he held himself, a quiet confidence that made Ben feel unsteady, aware of every misplaced thought and trembling nerve. He had caught himself staring more than once, drawn to the subtle roughness of Davenport's five o'clock shadow, the faint creases around his eyes that hinted at a life lived deliberately. It made Ben ache in a way he hadn't allowed himself to feel in years—a sharp, almost painful longing that left him breathless.

Now, as he lay on his mattress, with the thin sheet clinging to his skin, he felt that warmth spreading through him again, unsettling and exhilarating all at once. He closed his eyes, conjuring the image of Davenport's head tilted just so, the faint curl of his lips as if he held a private joke. Ben's pulse quickened, his breath catching in his throat. He reached up, pressing his palm against his chest where his heart thudded like a frantic drummer. His hand drifted lower, sliding beneath the waistband of his boxers, fingers brushing the warm, sensitive skin.

A low, involuntary moan slipped past his lips, half surprise, half yearning. His mind clung to the memory of Davenport's voice—measured, probing, each word carefully chosen, his hazel eyes never breaking their relentless gaze. Heat unfurled in his belly, fierce and insistent, his body straining against the mattress as he imagined Davenport's eyes fixed on him, unblinking, dissecting, owning every fragment of his vulnerability. His breaths came faster, his body trembling as he stroked himself through the thin fabric, the friction teasing him closer to the edge. He could almost feel Davenport's touch—imagined, yet so painfully real—firm, guiding, possessive. His moans grew louder, echoing off the bare walls, filling the cramped space with the sound of his surrender. His back arched, every muscle tightening, and for a brief, searing moment, the world narrowed to a single point of ecstasy, white, hot and overwhelming. He shuddered hard against the mattress, the tension unspooling in a wave that left him gasping, every nerve alight, his mind a blank, throbbing void.

As his body slowly relaxed, the aftershocks rolling through his limbs, Davenport's face remained etched in his mind, a ghostly imprint on the inside of his eyelids. Ben lay there, chest heaving, the room heavy with the scent of his release, and felt the slow, creeping return of the loneliness he had tried to banish. But this time, it felt different—less like a void and more like an ache, a wound he could no longer ignore.

When he returned for the second session, the world of the clinic felt tighter—like walls had subtly crept inward, the air thick with a palpable tension. He sat across from Davenport, and the silence between them crackled like live electricity. No ticking clock, no distant footsteps—only the undercurrent of two souls entwined in an unspoken duet. Sometimes, before speaking, Davenport would glance toward the door—as if checking for an audience, or for silence. One session, he'd said, almost as an aside, "No one really knows what happens in here but us." Ben had nodded then, but the words nested deep inside him, as though something unspoken had just taken root.

Ben always felt like he was on the periphery, a silent figure standing in the background of bright rooms or by the rugged rocks of a blustery coast. While other kids ran around laughing, their footsteps echoing on the worn, salty pavement as they played tag among the dilapidated stone walls, Ben stayed by the water's edge, a distant observer as he dug his small hands into the damp, gritty sand and stared at the distant line where ocean met sky. Ben realized early on that loneliness wasn't about being alone; it was about lacking a true connection with others.

In the weeks that followed, their sessions deepened into something dangerously intimate, slipping past the boundaries of professionalism like a whispered confession in a darkened room. What began as emotional excavation—digging through the cold, calcified layers of Ben's past—shifted into something more tactile, more visceral. The air between them grew heavier, thick with the scent of antiseptic and the unspoken weight of crossed lines. It felt as if the very walls of the studio leaned in, straining to capture each breath, each stuttered pause, each pulse of desire that crackled between them. Ben noticed the micro gestures first. A flash of warmth in Davenport's eyes, like the brief flicker of a candle in a draught, quickly extinguished but not unnoticed. There was an altered cadence in his voice, words that once cut clean now seemed to linger in the air, wrapping themselves around Ben's thoughts, pulling him closer to the edge of something he couldn't name. The gentle brush of Davenport's fingertips against paperwork, the way his gaze would trace the curve of Ben's jaw when he thought Ben wasn't looking—these moments burrowed into

Ben's mind, replaying in the quiet hours of the night, growing in significance with each cycle. And then there were the cracks, those rare, electrifying glimpses into the storm behind Davenport's calm façade. A sudden tightening of his jaw as Ben confessed to a particularly bitter memory, the faintest flicker of his eyes when Ben dared to meet them, a muscle tensing at his temple as if holding back a flood of unsaid things. These moments came and went like the flash of a predator's teeth—implying that beneath Davenport's polished surface lay something wild, something that could bite if provoked. Ben found himself counting the hours until each session, his mind occupied not by the mundane routine of his daily life, but by the unspoken exchanges that had come to define his days. He began memorizing every detail, cataloguing each tilt of Davenport's head, each sharp intake of breath, every slight adjustment of his posture as if trying to decipher a silent language only the two of them spoke. He became a collector of moments, storing them away like precious contraband, his heart quickening at the thought of each upcoming encounter.

Sometimes, Ben wondered if it was all in his head. But then Davenport's gaze would linger, a second too long, and doubt would vanish. Perhaps its warmth was just a professional habit, the lingering touch of fingers merely a byproduct of muscle memory. Maybe the tightness in his jaw was simply a reaction to a long day, a fleeting irritation, and not a signal meant for Ben alone. But then, in the next session, Davenport's eyes would linger a second too long, his hand would brush against Ben's knee as he reached for his notebook, and the doubt would crumble, replaced by a pulse of forbidden excitement that left Ben breathless. Their unspoken secret pulsed between them in every carefully measured pause, every loaded question. It felt like standing at the edge of a cliff, the wind pulling at his clothes, whispering of a fall that would shatter his bones and yet promise freedom in the brief, weightless descent. Would it save them both, or swallow them whole? The answer lay hidden in that silent charge between their bodies—an electric promise neither dared acknowledge, even so both felt in every stolen glance and every breathless confession. It drummed in the spaces between their words, in the silences that stretched just a heartbeat too long, in the knowing glances that neither had the courage to fully meet.

Was it all in his head? Perhaps. But perhaps not. And that ambiguity, that maddening, exhilarating uncertainty, only made the game even more irresistible.

~

Ben's earliest years unfolded on the razor's edge of the world that everyone else inhabited so naturally. Decades later, he would still feel like that boy—watching the world move without him. From that place he could hear the laughter of other children only as a faint echo, and it felt as if each giggle belonged to a life far beyond his reach. On the playground, their feet drummed against the gravel like carefree war drums, voices ricocheting off the metal bars of the jungle gym and lost in a sky too wide for him to claim. But there he stood in the margins, a slender, almost fragile figure swallowed by the swirl of roughhousing bodies. While his classmates spun around each other with effortless camaraderie, Ben's gaze turned inward. Behind his closed lids, worlds took shape—planets pirouetting in silent orbits, colossal dinosaurs lumbering across the asphalt in slow, thunderous strides, nostrils flaring in clouds of dust so vivid he could feel the ground shudder beneath each prehistoric foot.

Inside the classrooms, under the harsh, unblinking fluorescence, his difference became a beacon—one that drew uncomfortable curiosity from teachers and thinly veiled scorn from other students. The rigid rows of scratched wooden desks stretched before him like an unending line of soldiers at attention, and each time a teacher cleared her throat or tapped a clipboard, it felt like an order for him to conform. Their clipped instructions rattled around in the cavern of his mind, rarely landing with clarity. He tried to force his thoughts into their neat little boxes, but they leaked out at the seams, refusing to be contained. To his classmates, this odd detachment branded him a *weirdo*. They flung the word at him in whispered assemblies, as if it were a weapon sharp enough to cut him out of their circle.

Ben made earnest attempts to breach the invisible barrier. He memorized punch lines, mimicked gestures—waving an arm here, tossing a joke there—but every joke came out hollow, every gesture felt leaden. He watched his peers trade knowing glances or share secret smiles and marvelled at how effortlessly they fit together, like puzzle pieces he could never find. Each failed attempt at belonging only drove him deeper into the inner sanctum of his own mind, where words on paper became a portal to a world he could finally shape with precision and truth.

When he wrote, a blank sheet of paper transformed into a vast, hospitable landscape. He poured ink into the valleys of his thoughts, charting every hidden stream of feeling with startling clarity. His essays were raw, mercilessly honest—confessions laid bare. But to teachers who measured success by uniformity, his unguarded sincerity was a vulnerability to be sanitized. Their red pens scratched across his lines like surgeons' scalpels, excising anything that felt too fragile, too revealing. Their margin notes wrapped around his heart like a noose, tightening with each suggestion for "improvement."

He vividly recalled a school assignment one autumn morning when he was just nine. The homework seemed straightforward: describe your morning routine. He wrote about the golden light filtering through his bedroom curtains while his parent's fingers deftly guided each button into place, like a sacred ritual. He conveyed the quiet intimacy and the unspoken connection between parent and child. When he submitted the paper, he noticed a flash of something—was it disapproval or confusion in his teacher's eyes? Before he could fully grasp it, she leaned over his desk, her nails clicking as she unbuttoned his shirt. Her eyes silently demanded, "Can't you button your own shirt?" He felt the prickling awareness of many curious eyes on him as she sternly commanded him to button up himself. "Go on," her silence seemed to say. "Show them." His fingers fumbled at the buttons, each snap sounding like a tolling bell, broad-casting his embarrassment to the entire class. Music class offered no refuge, either. There, a single mispronounced lyric was enough to draw all eyes to him. The teacher halted the lesson, summoned him to stand beneath the blinding glare of the projector, and made him repeat the offending line until it fractured into an unrecognizable jumble of sounds. Around him, the classroom fell silent, swallowed by the echo of his own stammer. Each warped syllable reminded him of how strikingly he stood apart from the harmonious chorus of his peers.

Even the most benign efforts at social engi-neering served only to isolate him. The day the teacher announced a desk reshuffle—a well-meaning attempt to spark new friendships— Ben found himself exiled to the furthest corner of the room. His desk was encircled by a barri-cade of chairs and tables, a living dead zone that classmates christened "the Sargasso Sea," whispering the name as if it were a private joke he could never hope to understand. Each glance he dared cast around the crater that surrounded him revealed smirks and suppressed giggles, reinforcing the invisible walls that sealed him off from the world.

And yet, the deepest wounds came from moments when his innocence was twisted into a weapon against him. One restless afternoon in the gym, a makeshift baseball game—rubber ball, battered ruler bat—erupted with an energy he'd never felt before. Something galvanized him, and he found himself clutching the ruler with trembling anticipation. With one mighty swing, the ball soared upward, arcing toward the pale rafters in a moment of pure, suspended triumph. For an instant, the cheers that rose around him felt like warm silk draped across his shoulders. Then the ball took a cruel turn, striking a classmate in the eye with a hollow thud. Ecstasy curdled into panic. A sharp cry knifed the air, and before Ben could protest, the teacher stormed in, face pinched with outrage. Fingers jabbed at him. "He meant to do it," hissed someone. The teacher's voice cracked as she delivered her verdict: "If someone throws a rock at you, you throw a rock back at them." Her words hung heavy in the charged silence—law without mercy.

When he walked home that afternoon, the thundering memory of her decree buzzed in his ears like a swarm of bees. Rounding a corner, he froze at a scene he'd dreaded but somehow still felt unprepared for: a circle of classmates, their shadows long in the late afternoon light, fists tight around small, jagged stones. No warning came before the first rock struck. It hit his arm with a sharp kiss of pain, drawing blood. The next rock cracked against his shin. Then another found his shoulder. Dust and tears mixed on his scraped skin as he crumpled to the ground, backpack useless at his side. Their laughter chased him all the way into his shame, and when they finally dispersed, he lay trembling in a crater of chalky gravel, abandoned by the kindness he longed to believe might exist.

Years later, in the precisely arranged office of Davenport, Ben recited these memories with the practiced detachment of a narrator describing someone else's tale. He watched Davenport's face the way he once watched dinosaurs stomp across his inner playground, looking for a flicker of recognition. When he spoke about that day's walk home, Davenport's gaze slid down to Ben's lips for the briefest of moments, as if he saw in them the map of all the unsaid words and stifled cries. In that flash of eye contact, Ben felt something dangerous stir: the heady reminder that power could shift, even if only for an instant.

Leaning back in his chair, arms crossed, Ben allowed his voice to soften. "Have you ever wondered," he asked, "what it would feel like to... disappear?" His words fell into the silence between them, deliberate and low.

Davenport's head snapped up, the polished calm of his expression cracking like thin ice. "Disappear?" he repeated, his voice steady but his eyes flickering with surprise. "What do you mean by that?" Ben tilted his head, pressing his lips into a small, guarded smile—an expression that held both invitation and warning. "To let go of everything," he said. "To erase the past, the expectations, the cruelty. Start fresh. No ties. No responsibilities."

All at once the room seemed to grow smaller, the air between them heavy with unspoken possibilities. Davenport drummed his fingertips on the desk, jaw clenched in contemplation, and then, after a long moment, spoke in a voice that was both measured and charged with an odd, electric promise: "That's a compelling thought." Ben's lips curved a fraction higher as he leaned forward, eyes steady and bright with a glint of something unpredictable—an unspoken vow that this time, he would choose his own story.

~

Ben's centre had now shifted to the place enveloping Davenport in his routine, the walls that hugged him for hours, sometimes days, on end. Sterile, white, unfeeling walls that held the reverberation of countless whispered confessions, their blankness absorbing the quiet agony of every lost soul who crossed the threshold. But those same walls felt alive to Ben, pulsing with the faint charge of Davenport's presence, each surface witness to his every movement. Ben often wondered about

the other patients Davenport might see while
he wasn't there, each one given a share of that
intense, dissecting gaze, each one allowed to
occupy the same sacred space. A bitter, unspoken envy twisted in his chest at the thought of
those nameless, faceless others, their fears and
vulnerabilities splayed open for the doctor's
scrutiny. He imagined them—strangers shedding their secrets, their desperation, their
darkest confessions, while Davenport sat in
his high-backed chair, fingers tented, eyes
sharp and unrelenting, his presence a quiet
dominion over their fractured psyches. Ben's
stomach tightened at the thought, a primal
possessiveness he hadn't felt in years, a need
to reclaim his place at the centre of Davenport's attention. He resented the clock's steady
march, each second a step further from the
man's presence, the air growing thinner, his
own breath shallower as the door closed behind him at the end of each session. Within
his body, a countdown would reset each time,
longing to see him, to share the same air, to be
in the same space. The minutes in between
stretched into slow, agonizing eternities, the
world outside the studio a pale, muted thing

without the sharp, electric edge Davenport's presence lent it.

Ben noticed her the moment he stepped into Davenport's waiting room—Dr. Charlotte Petersen. She hovered just outside his vision, a pale wraith tethered to the therapist's orbit. Most session, she'd materialize at the rim of Davenport's studio window—half-shrouded, a silent sentry. His pulse clenched every time her face flickered into view, as if she were making sure Davenport never drifted from his appointed path. She had an almost preternatural knack for appearing exactly when his appointment time began, her entrance timed to the second. Once, Ben saw her debating quietly with Davenport, her voice sharp, her knuckles pale. He couldn't hear the words they'd exchanged, but the tension hung heavy in the air. He'd glimpse her golden hair catching the fluorescent lights, her posture immaculate as she glided down the hallway. She moved like a queen surveying her domain—effortless, unchallenged. Something in her precision unsettled him, a cold substratum he couldn't name. Who was she, really?
Then one afternoon, he found her perched in

his chair. Davenport introduced her with an offhanded "My partner, Charlotte," as though the words were as trivial as the weather. But to Ben, it was a thunderclap. The air quivered around her—she wasn't just a colleague, she ruled the room. When she rose to leave, her polished smile gleamed, and the scent of roses and lavender trailed after her like a ghost. He inhaled it, and for a moment, it felt as if she'd branded every surface, every corner of his mind.

My partner. The phrase wormed into Ben's gut, twisting and roiling like acid. Davenport didn't need to elaborate; his tone tightened around her name, his eyes drifting away. That barely imperceptible crack in his façade drove Ben wild. From then on, Charlotte became an obsession. Every time she drifted past the office—her heels clicking a metronome of control—he burned with a mix of resentment and fascination. She was perfect, too perfect: golden curls, flawless makeup, gowns tailored down to the last stitch, as though she existed to be admired.

She unnerved him—and drew him into an electrifying tension. She could laugh with a chilling stillness in her eyes, communicate in an unsettling silence. He scrutinized her every movement, desperate to decipher the armour that shielded her. And Davenport subtly tensed in her presence, a barely perceptible shift that only someone watching as intently as Ben would notice. That shift alerted Ben to a hidden depth, a silent threat lurking beneath. She moved with a calculated, deliberate grace, each step an assertion, every flick of her hair a rebellious challenge to the air that dared to touch her. Ben's gaze locked onto her sharp jawline, the way her lips pressed into a thin, resolute line as she scanned the room, her pupils narrowing dangerously in the dim light. This was her—the woman commanding Thomas's world, the whisperer in his ear, the fingers tracing the arms that had once cradled Ben in clandestine moments. For the first time, the adversary he hadn't known he faced revealed herself, a stunning, formidable mask hiding a force poised to consume the delicate illusion he had dared to claim as his own. She was a tempest in silk, a poised threat cloaked in meticulously chosen fabrics, her scent as potent and overwhelming as the first crack of lightning in a summer storm. Her gaze flickered his way, lingering a heartbeat too long, an enigmatic spark passing between them. Ben's heart pounded, his grip on the counter fastening as if he could anchor himself against the swelling tide of dread. She offered a polite, insincere smile, a slow, practiced curve of her lips that seemed to say, *I see you.*

It became a twisted game. Ben pored over every session, replaying every question Davenport asked, every syllable, every glance. On the surface, they looked like a power couple—successful, attractive, untouchable. But Ben felt the tension coiling between them, an invisible wire threatening to snap.
It wasn't jealousy. It was more invasive, like frost creeping under his skin. Ben felt banished, barricaded from something that should have been his. Soon, he wasn't just analysing their relationship—he was searching for a way in, a way to break Charlotte's hold, to displace her, to vanquish her and save Davenport.

Her mere presence reopened old scars, stirring a primal, almost childlike sense of rejection he couldn't shake. Ben had always been an outsider—an orphan adopted by a town that never quite knew what to do with him. Quiet and watchful, he learned early to blend into the background, to make himself small and invisible. It wasn't shyness, it was survival. Loneliness became his constant companion, shaping every thought and reaction. He made peace with it, convinced that some people were simply born on the fringes of everyone else's lives.

There were fleeting moments when he felt something more—when a teacher praised his schoolwork or a stray cat curled up in his lap, choosing him over everything else. Those tiny sparks of belonging took root in him, leaving a hunger for more that never quite faded. Even as an adult, he carried that ache: the quiet longing to be chosen, to be seen, to know that his presence really mattered. That's why Dr. Davenport unsettled him from their very first glance. The doctor looked at him like a puzzle worth solving, never glossing over his silences or half-finished thoughts. Davenport's focused attention felt like a balm, grounding him when he felt most adrift. For once, someone didn't look through him—someone actually saw him, and the effect was almost terrifying.

Then Charlotte entered the picture, gliding into Davenport's world with a confidence that struck a nerve he thought long dead. It wasn't just her beauty or graceful poise—it was deeper. She belonged to Davenport now— or rather, he belonged to her, the man who had begun to make Ben feel whole, and that truth twisted in his gut like a knife. Davenport—his secret obsession, the one who had pulled him out of lonely stupor—was already tethered to someone else. Ben imagined how Davenport's days now bent around Charlotte, how she wove herself seamlessly into his life. And Ben—with his quiet hopes and fractured soul— stood no chance against that. Charlotte wasn't just another woman; she embodied the completeness he'd always been denied, the effortless belonging that left him feeling abandoned once more.

He knew it was irrational. Charlotte had done nothing to him. Yet she was a reminder that he'd forever be the boy on the outside, watching happiness through a window and never quite touching it. Her presence shrank him back to that child who watched friendships bloom from the margins, longing to be invited in. He couldn't help but see her as an adversary—the woman who claimed the steady presence and guiding hand he'd only just begun to imagine for himself. Davenport was becoming his centre, and Charlotte threatened to shatter that fragile illusion.

One afternoon he lingered in the waiting area, pretending to scroll on his phone, while her laughter spilled from the slightly ajar door— bright, brittle, forced. The sound gnawed at him. What was Davenport seeing in her? He strained to catch fragments of conversation, but the words didn't matter—only the way she monopolized the air, her voice filling every crevice. When Davenport emerged to walk her to the lift, his grin was clipped, his gaze swinging past her to land on Ben—an electric flicker, charged with meaning. Not warmth. Something colder. As he guided her out, Davenport turned and said, "Come in." Smooth. Controlled. But the knife-edge beneath his calm was unmistakable.

Ben walked into his session under a hail of suppressed energy. He felt it now: Petersen wasn't just a girlfriend. She was an obstacle—

an impregnable fortress standing between him and everything he craved. And he would tear her down. Thomas stood beside her, but something in his posture made it look like he was leaning away. The distance between them wasn't in steps, but in energy—a subtle recoil Ben noticed like a sixth sense.

Days bled into identical greys. His life narrowed to those hour-long sessions. Work, colleagues, even sleep lost all substance. Only Davenport remained real. At night, he lay in pitch darkness, Davenport's measured voice looping in his head, a lullaby, and a curse. He replayed their exchanges ad nauseam, dissected every micro expression, wove them into a tapestry of obsession.
He found himself counting the minutes until he could sit opposite Davenport again, feel those calm, penetrating eyes on him. It wasn't therapy anymore; it never was. It was sustenance. Without it, he would drown.

He felt a subtle tremor coursing through his pulse, a gentle but persistent reminder that lingered long after each session. His cheeks flushed with warmth, a heat that spread under the surface of his skin, and he repeated to himself, like a mantra, that it was purely professional admiration—nothing more, nothing less. But, beneath that carefully constructed shield of reassurance, a conflicting storm brewed, a desire that smouldered quietly: the yearning to be significant, to be the one who truly caught Davenport's discerning eye.

This longing wrapped itself around him, weaving a delicate, intricate web of fantasies that occupied his thoughts. He found himself spiralling into scenarios painted in vivid detail. What if Davenport left Charlotte? What if he, with quiet bravery, could extricate Davenport from her stifling hold, liberating him and claiming him as his own? These musings unfolded slowly, each layer revealing itself with deliberate intensity, and in these imagined worlds, they stood side by side, in the aftermath of her absence—unburdened, open, and pure.

Nevertheless, despite the allure of these dreams, any doubt lingered, whispering insidiously. With each scenario he envisioned, a nagging uncertainty crept in, questioning whether it was even right to entertain such dreams, dreams that danced on the edge of possibility, igniting his mind with a slow-burning desire that refused to be extinguished.

~

Every mention of Charlotte became a blow. She didn't deserve Davenport. She didn't understand him like he did. He hated her for her perfection, her poise, for the way she seemed to own Davenport's world with a flick of her wrist. He convinced himself that Davenport was trapped in a gilded cage, bound by obligation, stifled by Charlotte's demands. He saw disgust in Davenport's eyes whenever her name surfaced—dark clouds brewing behind the calm. Ben became certain: Davenport was only pretending.

The thought began as a murmur: What if she weren't there? What if she simply... vanished?

It terrified him yet felt inevitable. Without her, Davenport could be free. Free to see Ben. Deep down, he knew it was monstrous—but the image excited him.

He tested the waters in his sessions, hinting at freedom, at the weight of burdensome attachments, watching Davenport's reactions. *His partner.* The phrase echoed in his skull. Soon, his daydreams spilled into meticulous planning. How? When? Each scenario unfolded. Ruthless, precise. It had to be flawless—for Davenport's sake. Ben's grip on reality weakened. Every exchange, every flicker of Davenport's expression, fuelled his resolve. He sat across from the man he adored, feigning progress in therapy, while scheming Charlotte's downfall. She had to go. It was the only path to his salvation—and, he believed, Davenport's.

The final pieces slid into place inside his fevered mind. He no longer wavered. Petersen would be erased. Only then could Davenport be truly free. And then—only then—Ben would have him entirely.

~

Ben's mind found no rest. Even in the dead of night, his thoughts refused to pause. While the streetlamps cut pale lines across his carpet, he'd lie awake on the thin mattress, heart hammering, as memories of every session with Davenport looped endlessly—an obsessive reel he could neither turn off nor rewind. Any fleeting mention of Petersen, any innocuous gesture Davenport made toward her, set off a fresh cascade of analysis. He'd never truly met Petersen, but in his mind, he'd already built her into something monstrous: a controlling force, a poison, the sole blockade between Davenport and his salvation.

He would pace the length of the room, arms wrapped around himself, murmuring into the stale air, She's dragging him down... She's poisoning his life... He pictured Petersen's face dissolving beneath the heel of his own relentless logic. Each syllable, a verdict. Each footstep, a countdown to her eradication. The moral fog that once slowed him had dissipated, replaced by an unblinking, surgical clarity. There was no debate about right or wrong. There was only the precise elimination of an obstacle.

In therapy, he began to reframe every exchange with Davenport as a calculated manoeuvre. Petersen became the immovable block, and death the unstoppable bulldozer. At first, Ben's interventions were subtle—an extra worn pause here, a carefully framed question there. He sowed his seeds quietly: "You mentioned something essential last week," he'd say, voice soft, eyes steady. "About releasing what holds you back." He watched, clinically delighted, as Davenport blinked, as his posture tightened, as Petersen's name seemed to lodge in his throat like a splinter. He planted ideas under the floorboards of their sessions, fleeing the conscious mind to fester in the hidden corners. "I used to think closeness meant safety," he observed one afternoon, "But sometimes it's the people right next to you that keep you stuck. Like... they might not mean to. But they do" His tone was earnest, almost gentle—designed to lull Davenport's defences. The slightest flinch in Davenport's expression, the brief quiver of his jaw, was proof the subterranean work was paying off. Ben chronicled each micro-shift in demeanour: the way Davenport's shoulders squared at the mention of liberation; the faint hitch in his breath when he hinted at Petersen's name; the covert tightening of his grip on the armrest. He transcribed these shifts into a ledger he kept in a battered notebook, drawing arrows and circles around every sign of fraying composure. Watching the idea of freedom twist and swell in Davenport's chest gave Ben a rush more intoxicating than any drug.

At the close of one session, as the clock hands edged toward the late afternoon lull, Ben struck with deliberate timing. The room was hushed save for the hum of the air conditioner. He leaned forward, voice low, confessional, as though baring his own wounds. "Do you ever feel," he asked, allowing the silence to drape around them, "I don't know. Like this isn't even your life? Like someone else wrote the script and forgot to tell you?" Davenport's blink was slow—careful. "What are you getting at?" he countered, lips tightening. Ben shrugged, brows lifting innocently, leaving Davenport purposely guessing as the air between them charged with unspoken danger. In that pregnant pause, Davenport finally exhaled the tension he'd been hoarding. "Life can be... complicated," he admitted, voice soft. "Sometimes," Ben said, inching forward as if sharing a secret, "the only way forward is to let go of whatever's weighing you down." He watched the flicker behind Davenport's neutral mask and recognized triumph in its depths. Another seed had taken root.

Outside the therapy room, he maintained the mask of professional calm. But inside, his psyche burned with purpose. His every waking hour he devoted to the eradication of Petersen. In the basement of his mind, he sketched dimensioned plans: potential surveillance, escape routes, possible contaminants or objects that left no mark, no trace. Night after night, he pored over toxicology journals, legal loopholes, accident reports that hinted at perfect plausibility. He built a dossier of alibis, wove timelines with surgical precision, and rehearsed the motions in the dark corridor of his apartment, shadowboxing in the silver light. He imagined her disappearance in eerie detail: the click of her apartment lock left open, the

slight stench of a forgotten chemical, the soft thud as she slumped to the floor with no one to hear her cry. He pictured Davenport's face upon discovering her absence—confusion, grief, but ultimately relief—his own hand there to steady him. In that afterglow, Ben would stand as the only pillar left intact, the selfless confidant guiding Davenport toward a brightness unshaded by Petersen's presence.
Ben's obsession grew insatiable.

Even as he painstakingly mapped out every move—each step a cog in the immaculate machinery of his mind—Ben felt a tremor of uncertainty beneath the dark thrill of control. Desire and determination blurred into one intoxicating alloy, but somewhere in the back of his racing thoughts, a faint voice whispered of cost and consequence. He had always craved order, a sense of justice life had never afforded him. He'd dreamed of a saviour to pull him from the hailstorm of rocks his classmates once hurled, their jagged edges carving scars into the soft shell of his boyhood. Yet no one had come. No hand had reached through that cold, clattering darkness. Instead, he'd learned that the world obeyed only cruel, indifferent rules: the strong crush the weak, no questions asked.

Now, though, he would be the one to intervene, he told himself that with desperate conviction, but doubt gnawed at him. If he unleashed his will on Petersen, what would remain of his own soul? He imagined Davenport as a man trapped in invisible bars of compromise and quiet despair, Charlotte Petersen the jailer with her bright smile and sharper words. He would shatter those chains, fling open the door, guide Davenport back into the light. He would be the liberator, steady and precise, a quiet force moving with purpose rather than violence. And yet what if he became the monster he'd always feared? What if the scales of justice tipped too far?

Still, the vision of Davenport's hollow eyes, the way they'd flicker with relief, propelled him forward. In his mind, Ben rehearsed the moment: the lock clicking open, the chains falling away, the sudden gasp of freedom. He saw himself as the steady hand in the dark, the murmur in the storm, the constant amid a shifting world. But beneath that image lurked a shadow: the ghost of every rule he'd broken to get here, the outline of every moral line he was about to cross.

In that charged instant, his heart pounded with electric certainty and aching conflict. He could taste both triumph and terror, as if two futures fought within him. Would he stand beside Davenport as the compassionate guide he envisioned, or discover that the real bondage was in his own thirst for power? The contours of his destiny had already begun to form, but uncertainty thrummed at their edges: no loose ends, no questions asked, he had promised himself. And so, his mind rattled with the questions he could not silence.

Soon, Petersen would be gone. And in the vast emptiness left behind, he would wait—ope-armed and unwavering, or broken by the weight of what he'd done. In his chest, the ticking clock of fate counted down, each second a challenge: could he live with the truth of who he was about to become?

~

The moment Ben swung open the battered wooden door of the tiny corner fish shop tucked between a bakery and a hardware store in town, the air struck him like a wave: a bracing, salty gust, mingling faintly with the bakery's sweetness and the hardware store's earthy scent that carried the cold, coppery tang of freshly gutted fish and the faintest undercurrent of seaweed. In the worn threshold—slab creaked beneath his boots, announcing his arrival as the single fluorescent tube overhead flickered, its hum a low, steady drone in the near-silence. Pale light washed across row upon row of gleaming ice beds— long, stainless troughs heaped with silver— scaled specimens whose slick bodies caught every sparkle, each droplet of meltwater refracting into tiny prisms. In one corner, wooden crates, stencilled with last week's batch barcodes, sat heaped with mussels and clams, their ridged shells still slick and briny from the morning's haul. Outside, the faded, peeling sign hung crooked above the glass paned window: a handwritten invitation so weatherworn it barely registered to wandering tourists. But to those who lived here, it was a sacred waypoint, the place they came for their evening meal, trusting Ben's steady hands more than any recipe book or restaurant. He stepped behind the counter and reached instinctively for his filleting knife. Its handle fit his palm like muscle memory; the weight balanced just right—precise, dependable. There was a comfort in the motion: slit, gut, scrape. Not messy, not cruel. Just necessary.

Inside, the world settled into its usual routine. Ben had been a fishmonger since he was eighteen, embracing a new way of life that differed from what he was used to. It was a method to cope with the heavy burden of leaving his childhood behind and stepping into adulthood—another time when Ben had to grow up too soon, after losing his sole parental figure to a stubborn illness that both had been too proud to fully acknowledge. It was his escape from that summer when everything changed suddenly. Before then, Ben had never even handled a fish, despite his father's unsuccessful attempts. He would often say, "It's a life skill. When I was a kid, it was a necessity," eventually giving in to Ben's preference for the quiet corner of his room, where he could lose himself in books about planets or tectonic plates. Those Sundays by the water were gone now, along with the memory of his father's voice. A voice that had resonated in his ears for most of his life shouldn't be forgotten so quickly. Yet, Ben was losing it, and he resented himself for it. So he pushed these thoughts to the back of his mind, where hazy memories were stored, far from reach, where all the other worldly noises awaited erasure in Ben's lifelong pursuit of tranquillity, protection, and safety.

Ben moved with the confidence of muscle memory: his shoulders bore the familiar ache of routines performed through countless mornings, and his fingers instinctively curled around tools designed for a single purpose. His gaze swept across the counter until it rested on his knife—a slender, razor-sharp blade with a handle worn matte from years of use. He picked it up and felt a familiar thrill, a subtle hum of anticipation tingling at his fingertips. Leaning forward, he pressed the blade against the first fish—a sleek, silver cod—and with hardly more resistance than a painter's

brush gliding over canvas, he guided the steel
through flesh and bone. Scales scattered like
morning snow on ice: flecks of grey and silver
falling onto the bed, shimmering like stardust.
Each cut was careful, exacting: the fillet peeled
away in a single, graceful arc, leaving translucent flesh stretched and unblemished. He
paused to discard fins and ribs, stripping away
membranes that held unnecessary moisture,
until only neat, pale steaks remained—flesh so
firm and pink it could have passed for porcelain under the shop's stark light. Ben arranged
them in a row on a chilled plate; their edges
caught the glare of the fluorescent bulb like
trophies of his craft. To him, knives were not
simple tools but extensions of his will: each
one demanding respect, each one carrying its
own balance, its own weight in his hand, waiting for the patient minute that would unlock
its promise.

Ben rarely spoke. Over his shoulder, the low
murmur of customers drifted: rough-hewn
fishermen in rubber boots trading jesting
complaints about the fickle weather, young
couples planning weekend barbecues with the
brittle enthusiasm of the untested, mothers

corralling squirming children away from the ice beds. Words tumbled free-cracked jokes, forced pleasantries, yet Ben's lips remained sealed. He offered only a curt nod, his eyes never wavering from the blade. A deft slice, a precise fillet, a wrapped order handed over the counter in crisp paper: it was a ritual practiced so many times that it felt older than him, older than the peeling paint on the doorframe. Then he would wipe his hands on his apron, leer at nothing in particular, and watch as their footsteps carried them back into the world beyond his glass.

When the clock struck noon, Ben slid out the back door and into the narrow alley that led to the bench by the shore. The path was tight, paved with uneven cobbles that whispered beneath his soles, and flanked by weather-beaten walls stained with salt. At the end lay his perch: a simple plank of driftwood, bleached by sun and scarred by countless storms, anchored on squat posts driven into the sand. He settled there, legs splayed, breathing in the vastness. Before him, the beach stretched in a widowed arc: damp sand where waves drew lazy crescents of foam before sighing back into the sea. The water was a shifting canvas with smudges of slate, swirls of cobalt and pewter captured beneath a sky mottled by running clouds. Overhead, gulls wheeled and cried, riding invisible currents as though pitted against the wind itself.

Ben welcomed these moments of quiet. The wind stung his cheeks with salt, sharp enough to taste on his tongue, and he let the cold bite anchor him in the present. His mind remained a restless tide, churning with thought. He watched the few souls who ventured close to the water: a couple wandering hand in hand, the man's straw hat tilted over his brow, the woman's laughter a brittle chime that faded under the sea's roar; children darting after wheel-tipped gulls, squealing as their sugar-dipped cones melted in the sun; tourists arrayed along the shoreline, cameras clicking frantically in a vain attempt to capture nature's indifference. To Ben, their motions felt rote, as though they were actors following an unseen script, their joy a fragile gesture laid over the sea's eternal indifference.

His lunch—a simple sandwich swathed in wax paper—sat untouched at his side, half-buried in a handful of sea grass. He stared at it, hunger evaporated by the emptiness he couldn't fill. Eating felt mechanical; a routine as flat as the steady slice of his knife. Better to let the ache in his stomach remind him that he was alive—that beneath each breath, each heartbeat, a fragile reminder that something still mattered. Somewhere, beyond his careful detachment, that tether kept him from drifting entirely into himself. Beneath his bench, the sea himself made no promises or threats. He rose and fell as he willed, heedless of human longing. Dark currents churned beneath the surface, hidden from those who marvelled at the glittering crests. In this cold certainty Ben found a brittle solace: in the sea's indifference he recognized a shadow of his own distance. Peace eluded him, but in the ocean's unsentimental rhythm lay a mirror for his quiet acceptance. The tide would turn; the sea would bring fresh harvest to his doorstep in the morning; new fish would gleam like jewels under fluorescent light. The world would go on as it must, indifferent to his private anguish or desire.

When the ghost of the lunch bell tolled inside

his skull, Ben pushed himself up and retraced his steps down the alley to his own little kingdom. The door groaned on its rusty hinges, spilling that briny, raw-fish perfume around him like a familiar cloak. He slipped behind the counter as easily as pulling on a second skin—the knife's cool steel fitting snugly in his grip, the ice beds shimmering with their promise of quiet, precise labour. The steady thud of blade on cutting board, the gentle give of flesh under steel: it was a ritual that always soothed the restless swirl inside his head.

Almost on cue, the tiny shop bell rang out, clear and insistent. Ben lifted his eyes. There stood Davenport—tall, composed, trench coat draping him like a mantle of command, polished boots tapping out authority on the tile— and just behind him, Petersen in her riot of clashing prints. Today her hat was an extravagant display of ribbons, a burst of colour utterly at odds with the subdued slate and silver of fish and frost.
"Good afternoon," Davenport said, voice smooth as sea-worn stone, offering that slow, knowing smile that had once sent warmth through Ben's chest—and now only left an

ache. Petersen paused in the doorway, wrinkling her nose at the fish counters as if their scent were an affront. "Oh," she said in clipped, breathy tones, "perhaps not seafood today." Her brow lifted triumphantly, as though she'd saved him from some grim fate. Ben caught the brief flicker of annoyance in Davenport's eyes before he straightened his expression into polite formality. Davenport's smile didn't quite reach his eyes when Charlotte spoke. There was a pause—half a second, no more—but in it, Ben sensed a gap. Not anger. Not resentment. Something colder. Boredom? "Another time, Ben," he murmured softly, empty as shells tossed by the tide. Petersen slipped her arm through his, head tilted in triumph, and together they drifted back out, leaving behind a wave of stale perfume and self-satisfaction.

The bell chimed again as the door closed, and the shop fell into a hush so deep it sucked the hum from the lights. Ben stayed rooted at the counter, staring at the empty threshold as if expecting them to reverse course at any moment. His heart hammered in his temples, every beat a staccato reminder of the sudden, disorienting spike of anger and loss when he saw her arm reaching over Davenport's.

Without realizing it, his hands returned to the fish. He liked the smallness of the act. Taking something whole and reducing it to parts. The neatness of it. The fish's head came off cleanly in a single stroke. The silver skin peeled back like paper. People flinched at the sight. Ben didn't. There was a kind of reverence in it. Like undoing something nature had built, just to prove he could. The blade whispered through soft flesh in its familiar rhythm—but his mind was jagged, his pulse racing, and the next moment his grip tightened too far. The knife slipped, slicing the tip of his finger. He froze only when the hot sting arrived, a second too late. A pristine red line bloomed against pale skin, a single drop quivering before splashing onto the steel counter. Ben inhaled sharply, copper flooding his mouth in that metallic tang he'd learned to crave. Pain flared, sharp and anchoring, and he welcomed every throbbing pulse—it proved he was alive, kept him tethered as his thoughts threatened to drift away in the storm. He watched, nearly entranced, as the blood smeared into pale grey metal, spoor of his anger etched in thin, furious lines.

His good hand went to his chest, fingers finding the rough bandage on his other hand—an old wound that never fully healed, a souvenir from a late-night haul. With deliberate care he peeled back the rag, letting the razor pain lance through him again. Then he paused, took a breath, and set about wrapping fresh gauze around the cut, movements precise despite the tingling edge of adrenaline.

As he wound the bandage tight, his mind locked onto a single, burning image: Petersen's smug, triumphant smile as she lured Davenport away, her false sweetness suffocating him.

He pictured it then. How easily it could happen. A slip. A single, well-timed strike. The museum she kept mentioning, with its high ceilings and silent galleries. All it would take was a moment alone. No screams. Just breath caught in surprise, her body crumpling soundlessly beside a shattered exhibit. People would assume it was an accident—they always did when elegance met tragedy. No one would suspect the quiet man who kept to himself,

who knew exactly when to disappear.
 Holding the cool steel of his knife in his
hand—this same blade that carved through
fish so effortlessly— a slow, measured smile
curled his lips. In that steady weight lay order,
precision, and a promise as sure as the turning
tide.

~

Later that day, when Ben stepped back into
Davenport's office, the air around them crackled as if a live wire had been stretched taut between two poles. The amber light from the
desk lamp caught in the fine dust motes drifting above a pile of files. Davenport sat rigid
behind his desk, shoulders squared, knuckles
white as he gripped his pen. Across from him,
Ben leaned forward, elbows planted on the
edge of the desk, as though he intended to pry
open Davenport's very soul. "Ever feel like
you're... disappearing?" he murmured one afternoon, low and dangerous, each word

measured yet laced with the promise of violence.

The events of that afternoon before lingered like a bitter aftertaste. Davenport appearing at his workplace—an unsolicited invasion of his space, a trespass into the one corner of the world where Ben felt grounded—had shaken him. It was a reminder that Davenport existed beyond the confines of his studio, a life lived beyond the filtered light and hushed tones of their sessions. But, in that moment, he hadn't been alone. Petersen had been there, her bright, clashing colours and sharp, knowing smile trailing behind him like an unwanted spectre, reminding him of the life Davenport shared with someone else. It left Ben feeling as though he were slowly fading into the background of his own existence, a shadow slipping behind the scenes, an extra in a life he had once dared to imagine as his own.

For the first time, he truly understood the depths of his own irrelevance, the bitter knowledge that he had never been the main character in his own story—merely a ghost haunting the periphery, waiting for someone else's attention to solidify his form.

Ben's gaze tightened on Davenport's face, searching for the man he had idolized, the one he'd learned to love in stolen glances and whispered confessions.

Davenport's hand stuttered, the pen halting mid-sentence. He looked up, pupils shrinking, face pale beneath the overhead lamp. "Disappearing how?" he asked, voice clipped, guarded. A tremor ran through his fingers, betraying the calm he strove to project. Ben allowed a slow, bitter smile to spread across his lips, dark amusement glinting in his eyes. "I mean losing yourself in the very things you think are saving you—your work, your routines... people, especially." He let the last word hang between them like a guillotine blade. That flicker of unrest in Davenport's gaze—furtive, exhausted—was all the invitation Ben needed. He pressed on, voice dropping even lower. "What if those people are nothing but chains around your soul?" The question cut deeper than any scalpel. Davenport's pen snapped shut with a muted crack, and he brushed a hand through his hair, his breath coming in tight little bursts. "People... yeah. They complicate things more than they fix them." he answered at last, tone controlled but brittle, as if he'd cracked thin porcelain. "Or maybe," Ben whispered, leaning so close Davenport could smell the faint tang of Ben's cologne, "we just let them stay too long." There—just for a heartbeat, Davenport's defences sagged. His shoulders slumped, a fine line creased the corner of his mouth, and his eyes darted back to meet Ben's, raw and unguarded. It was a look Ben recognized, a look he had seen in his own reflection on countless, lonely nights—a look of exhaustion, of quiet, unspoken resentment.

Davenport's lips parted as if to speak, a muscle in his jaw flexed, and for that brief, electric second, Ben felt the silent, unspoken agreement pass between them. It was the barest flicker, the smallest hint of an unspoken truth, but Ben seized on it, like a blade finding the perfect angle to cut. Then, as quickly as it had come, the moment was gone. Davenport straightened, but the movement lacked conviction. His shoulders lifted as if by habit, not strength. For a split second, Ben thought he saw it—that hollowed look of a man who's been holding himself together for too long. He swallowed, his Adam's apple bobbing in a tight, calm motion, and his eyes shuttered, locking Ben out once more. The air in the room thickened, the strained silence closing in around them like a vice, and the world seemed to tilt ever so slightly, the shadows in the corners of the room growing darker, more conspiratorial.

But Ben had registered the signal, the faint, trembling crack in the man's facade, the barely perceptible confirmation that had slipped through in a moment of weakness.

It began as a look. As silence stretched between their words and something in that stillness held a promise, Ben knew, neither dared name. By the end of their session, Ben's plan had coagulated into something cold and undeniable. The guilt had curdled into resolve long before that night—each encounter with Petersen sharpening it further. Each session with Davenport until that point had left him more certain of the contours of his intent, sharpening his focus until every thought circled back to one inevitable conclusion. In Davenport's exhaustion, he saw confirmation—and in Petersen, he saw the final piece to be removed. A faint salt taste touched his tongue then, sudden and phantom, as if summoned by memory. He didn't question it. Some things left their mark without sound, without words.

He remembered the afternoon with vivid clarity: Ben's pulse fluttered with the sting of the fresh cut on his finger as he crouched in the cramped back room, wrapping his wound in gauze with the efficiency of someone long acquainted with minor injuries. As he pulled the bandage tight, the muffled sound of voices drifted through the thin partition wall. At first, just a low, indistinct murmur, but then clearer, sharper, cutting through the dense, salty air like a blade through flesh.
"Why do you always do this?" Davenport's voice, clipped and tight, punctuated by the sharp clack of his polished shoes against the tile. "We had a plan. Seafood risotto, a nice bottle of white, fresh herbs—I went out of my way to make it special. And you just dismiss it like it's nothing."
Petersen's response came quick, a smooth, practiced tone layered with just enough edge to draw blood. "Oh, for God's sake, Thomas. I simply changed my mind. It's just a dinner,

not a grand gala. You're always so dramatic."

"I'm dramatic?" Davenport's voice spiked, a hint of real heat breaking through his normally calculated tone. "I'm trying to do something nice for our friends, and you can't even respect that? You can't just—" He cut himself off, the sharp intake of breath audible even from the back room. Ben stilled, his fingers frozen mid-wrap as he strained to hear every word. Petersen's heels clicked as she shifted her weight, the sound like gunshots in the otherwise silent shop. "Respect?" she echoed, her tone dripping with disdain. "You're the one caring more about appearances than about what I actually want."

There was a pause, thick and crackling, the air between them seeming to compress. Ben imagined Davenport's jaw tightening, his shoulders squaring like a boxer in the ring. The man had always struck him as someone who craved control, a steady hand in a world spinning out of balance.

"Fine," Davenport snapped, his voice suddenly lower, more dangerous. "Do you want to change the rest of the plans, too? Or is it too early for you to decide?"

"Oh, don't start," Petersen shot back, her voice sharp enough to flay skin. "The museum tour is still at nine. I'm not some tyrant, Thomas, despite what you like to tell yourself."

~

Ben was intimately familiar with the Escape Room Museum, knowing every narrow hallway, concealed nook, and deceptive wall by heart. As a child, he had worked there after school, captivated by its mysterious allure where the chaos of the outside world was replaced by the structured logic of puzzles. The museum was housed in an old mansion, transformed by an eccentric Italian immigrant, with each room meticulously crafted with tight corridors, hidden compartments, and clever misdirection intended to baffle even the most astute visitors. Ben mastered its intricacies, fixed aging props with his skilled hands, and

delighted in the sound of smoothly function-
ing gears. Years later, when it had become
nothing more than a tourist attraction, he
could still find his way through it blindfolded,
feeling the damp stones as easily as he would
his own palm. Here, surrounded by locks and
levers, he felt sharp and vibrant—he felt at
home.

Later, in the hush of his modest flat, the late
afternoon sun slanted through drawn curtains,
painting the floorboards with long, yawning
shadows. The town's distant hum filtered
through the windowpane, and Romeo—sleek,
black, with eyes like polished emerald—
perched on the sill, silent sentinel. Ben
dropped his keys onto the small hallway table,
loosened his collar until the fabric fell away
from his throat, and let the dull ache of obsession settle itself across his chest like a smoth-
ering blanket. Here, in this half-light, his plan
felt inevitable.
He drifted into the kitchenette, knife in hand,
and began slicing a salad for dinner. Romeo
hopped onto the counter, curved against Ben's
arm, rubbing his sleek body against the cool

steel. "You get it, don't you?" Ben murmured; voice raw with something like reverence. The cat's tail flicked once, inscrutable—a question or maybe a purr of complicity. Ben envied that feline simplicity: no guilt, no schemes, only the moment's quiet joy.

8:00 pm. They'd be exchanging pleasantries and compliments by now, full from a delicious, non-seafood dinner. Probably not even homemade—Petersen would've dragged them out to some restaurant instead, changing Davenport's plans without a second thought.
He rose and began to pace the narrow living room, anticipation coiling tighter around his lungs with every step. Romeo followed, tail held high, as if judging each turn. Ben's heart pounded in his throat as he traced the museum's labyrinthine layout on an invisible map: one clean slice here, a swift cut there, and his design would come to blooded fruition.
At the window he stopped, forehead pressed to the cool glass, streetlamps flickering on like distant beacons unaware of the storm brewing below. Romeo leapt to the floor and brushed

against his ankle, seeking affection. Ben knelt, running fingers through the cat's silken fur, every scratch behind the ears a vow of benevolence he would soon betray. "Don't worry," he whispered, voice trembling. "I'll be fine."
The cat purred, blind to tomorrow's promise, trusting the hand that stroked him. Ben rose once more, heart hammering: 8.15pm. Everything was in motion. In minutes he would slip into that twisting maze of puzzles, meld into the shadows he knew so intimately, and wait. Petersen would never know what awaited her until it was too late. And when the final piece clicked into place, Davenport would be free—untethered, reborn in the dark aftermath.

Ben turned away from the window, finding the apartment suddenly oppressive. Romeo observed quietly, a mute witness to the impending tragedy. Ben took a deep, deliberate breath, the sense of unavoidable fate pressing down on him like a burial cloth. He grabbed his coat, and stepped into the night, leaving behind a silence-laden apartment. Outside, the world continued its motion, unaware, until Ben would trigger a new, darker chapter. He paused at the door before leaving then left it slightly ajar for Romeo to find its way into that new world. "You're going to live forever," he whispered, giving the cat one last, longing look.

~

The museum crouched at the end of a narrow, cobbled alley; its crooked, soot-stained stones framed by the jagged shadows of overhanging gables. Iron-bound windows, fogged with decades of grime, caught the last glimmers of daylight, their dull glass reflecting only the flicker of gas lamps lining the lane. A wrought-iron gate creaked in the evening breeze, its hinges whispering ghost stories to the chill air, while the briny tang of the nearby harbour mingled with the earthy musk of damp stone. Ivy clung to the crumbling façade, its twisting tendrils reaching for the pitted masonry like skeletal fingers. Above the arched entrance, a tarnished brass plaque, letters worn smooth by years of rain and grasping hands, read simply:

Escape Room Museum.
Once a grand townhouse, the building had half-collapsed in a devastating fire decades before, flames licking through its upper floors like a starving beast. Survivors wove the remaining shell together with modern stone, glass, and steel, rebirthing the ruin as the country's first escape room attraction and, later, its peculiar museum. The result was an eerie, disjointed structure, caught between eras and haunted by its own violent rebirth. In recent years, the museum leaned into this mythos—candlelit tours, ghost story nights, and invented tragedies about the wealthy couple lost in the blaze. Ben knew it was all marketing: musty curators spinning tales of lost love and tragic death to lure in macabre tourists and squeeze a last drop of profit from a fading relic.

His pulse fluttered beneath his skin like a war drum as he approached the entrance, the iron gate clanging shut behind him with a reverberation that seemed to shake his bones. A damp, breathless chill enveloped him as he stepped inside, low ceilings and narrow corridors pressing in, as if the building resented its second life. Flickering lanterns hung from iron brackets, casting long, writhing shadows that quivered with every movement. The damp air carried a sour hint of mildew and old regret. Beneath his feet, warped oak floorboards groaned, their ancient joints creaking in protest as he ventured deeper. Dust motes floated in the amber lamplight like suspended souls, their ghostly dance stirring memories of forgotten whispers and hurried footsteps. Behind a glass case, an antique clockwork mechanism shuddered to life—reluctant gears clicking and sighing. Tonight's experimental late-night opening aimed to draw fresh blood into the museum's aging veins. A handful of tourists shuffled through the stone corridors, hushed voices echoing against the walls, occasional nervous laughter slicing the silence like a blade. A dark-haired guide in a long, waxed coat led a small group toward the grand staircase, his lantern casting frantic shadows as he spun yet another fabricated tale of the house's tragic past, his voice lilting through the gloom like a ritual chant.

Ben slipped into a side passage, his pulse hammering in his ears as he followed the faint echoes of familiar voices. The stone walls grew more uneven here, plaster flaking away to reveal fire-scorched masonry beneath. He paused beneath a crumbling archway, its cracked keystone stained by decades of seepage, and drew a ragged breath, lungs burning in the frigid air.

To his left, a poorly lit backdoor offered escape to a hidden garden. To his right, a stout oak door bore a tarnished brass plaque—its edges darkened by countless hands—that read: Escape Room 102 – The Mineral Maze. The letters gleamed ominously in the dim light, each etched character a silent dare. Beyond the door, he heard the faint murmur of other visitors progressing upstairs, the muffled scrape of shoes on flagstones, and the soft, haunting strum of classical guitar from hidden speakers, meant to lull guests into a false calm.

Then he saw them.

In the amber glow of the next gallery, Davenport and Petersen stood close, alone, locked in a private world. Petersen leaned toward him, her slender finger sketching an unseen line across his forearm. Her hat rested at her hip, haloed by the warm light. Sunlit strands of honey-gold hair spilled over her shoulder; her lips curved into that careless, delighted smile Ben had once thought belonged only to him. The sight sent a serpent of rage coiling up his spine, his vision tunnelling until cornices and columns dissolved into an obsidian tunnel of focus.

It should have been me, he thought, muscles tensing as he cautiously moved forward, concealing himself behind one of the room's tapestry curtains. His teeth ground together, sending a metallic tang coursing across his tongue. Behind him, the low hum of fluorescent bulbs and the soft chatter of patrons blurred into a single droning pulse.

Davenport looked up and frowned, catching Ben off guard, prompting him to pull back in fear of being discovered. Davenport then moved aside to take a phone call and disappeared into the darkness just beyond the museum's main entrance. Meanwhile, Petersen stood in the middle of that mineral maze room, completely unaware of the predator lurking in the shadows. His opportunity had come.

Ben took a deep breath, detecting the artificial desert aroma pumped into the exhibit: dry, sharp, unsettling. He pushed the curtain aside and leaped into the Mineral Maze. Heat-simulating lamps bathed the room, creating jagged shadows on the floor as if the space itself was split. Tables covered with rough, sand-coloured cloths displayed trays of minerals—quartz, amethyst, and pyrite clusters that sparkled like stars trapped in a cage. At the centre, a polished wooden table showcased desert roses—gypsum formations with sharp, blade-like edges, each petal curled into a fragile, alien bloom.

Canvas tents drooped overhead like old sails, their folds hiding secrets, while brass oil lamps cast amber light, forming a flickering mirage against the decorated walls. Murals of sun-bleached dunes and swaying palms covered the room in ochre and emerald hues, evoking an endless horizon buried under a relentless sun. Worn leather saddlebags, coiled ropes, and sand-coated canteens hung from the tent poles, relics of a bygone expedition. The air vibrated with the gentle hum of hidden fans, spreading the dry, dusty scent of stone

and burning sand throughout the space.
Under a domed canopy painted with drifting
clouds and beaded fronds, a circular stone
pedestal stood in the room's centre, its surface
scattered with gypsum shards, polished obsidian, and sandstone fragments. Here, visitors
were invited to touch the rocks, to experience
the ancient, crumbling textures of a world long
entombed beneath the moving sands. He
drifted forward, drawn by a dark impulse. His
pulse throbbed in his temples. He paused at
the low display, nestled among them, a jagged
shard of obsidian, about the size of a fist.
Only a few paces separated them now. Petersen's beam of attention remained fixed on
the exhibits—on dust-encrusted glass and
chipped fossils—completely unaware of the
shadow gliding toward her. Ben's breath
slowed, becoming deliberate, measured. He
felt the shard's weight as a forbidden cove-
nant, a pact sealed in the coiling tendrils of
hate.
Then the spell broke.
Ben's hand shot to the table beside him with
the speed of a striking viper, his fingers
clenching around the jagged petals of a desert

rose—a lethal cluster of mineral blades sharp enough to slice flesh like butter if gripped too tightly. He felt the sharp bite of the desert rose gouge into his palm, igniting a searing pain as he swung his arm back with ferocious intent. He lunged forward with unrestrained fury, launching the obsidian through the oppressive air without hesitation. He brought the rock down in a tight arc, swift and silent. It met Petersen's skull with a wet, cracking thud that echoed like a judgment, brutal and irreversible. The sound reverberated with the power of distant thunder, a harbinger of doom. Her gasp died in her throat, frozen mid-exhale, consumed by a sudden, bone-chilling silence. She crumpled to the ground in a lifeless heap, the straw hat falling beside her with a hollow thud, like a wounded bird plummeting from the sky.

Charlotte fell like porcelain figure shattered against marble. She had been cornered beneath the jagged arch of the mineral maze, her breath coming in ragged, panicked gasps, her polished heels slipping against the dusty stone floor. The dim, flickering emergency lights cast their shadows in frantic, disjointed arcs, elongating their limbs into grotesque, writhing shapes against the rust-streaked walls. She had clawed at the air, her manicured nails scraping against the rough, weathered stone, her cries for help swallowed by the thick, damp air that clung to the museum's lower galleries like a shroud.

Ben had stepped into the light, his face a pale, ghostly blur in the half-darkness, his eyes locked on hers with a cold, unblinking intensity. He had moved slowly, deliberately, each step echoing the final, leaden beats of her heart. She had stumbled backward, her shoulder striking the sharp edge of a rusted iron support beam, her polished hair falling in wild, tangled strands across her face as her legs gave way beneath her. Her veins hummed with the static of panic, her breath catching in her throat as the reality of her situation closed around her like a vice.

He had reached for her then, his fingers curling around the delicate, spiralling edges of the fossilized desert rose, its sharp, crystalline petals cutting into his palm as he tightened his grip. He had felt the jagged edges bite into his skin, the weight of the fossil steady in his palm. As he swung with precision, the first blow struck her across the temple. The sharp mineral tore through flesh, splintered bone. The sound rang out like the snapping of something vital. Her head jerked to the side, lips parting in a breathless gasp, eyes wide and uncomprehending as pain bloomed behind them in a blinding, agonizing white.

He had struck her again, the jagged, spira-shaped stone crashing into the side of her head with a dull, wet thud, the impact reverberating through his arm, up into his shoulder, and down into the pit of his stomach. Somewhere overhead, the faint melody of exotic birdsong continued, grotesquely serene. He stood, chest heaving, staring at the obsidian shard now smeared with dark flecks. An uncertain triumph lodged in his throat, quickly seized by a crushing realization: this was no deliverance but an unthinkable damnation. The fossil slipped from his blood-slick fingers, clattering to the floor with a sharp, ringing clang, its once delicate petals now streaked with dark, rust-red stains.

Time splintered. In the stunned, adrenaline-fueled instant, Ben saw blood bloom across her skin, deep crimson sliding down her temple, catching the lamplight like a fell jewel. Her lashes fluttered once, then stilled. Her body went limp, folding into the coarse, sandy floor of the exhibit. She had crumpled to the floor, her limbs folding beneath her like a broken marionette, her blood pooling around her in a dark, spreading halo that seeped into the cracks between the uneven stones. Her eyes had rolled back into her head, her breath rattling in her throat, her body twitching and spasming as the last, desperate pulses of life drained from her shattered form.

And then, at last, the silence had descended.

Hands quaking so hard he thought his bones might shatter, Ben stumbled backward. Charlotte's body lay crumpled at his feet, golden hair matted with dark, congealing blood. The iron tang of it flooded his nostrils, sharp and insistent. For a moment time fractured. His chest heaved; his vision blurred as the flickering light threw monstrous shapes onto the walls. Then he saw the bookshelf. Bulging with dusty tomes and strange relics, it loomed like a gaunt sentinel. One leather-bound volume, its spine scored by age and stamped with a coiled serpent, jutted out as though begging to be freed.

Ben crossed the room in three desperate strides, the air thick with the stink of blood and fear. He seized the book's cold, cracked spine, the oak grain bit into his palms. A soft, mechanical click reverberated beneath him. Gears groaned, and the shelf trembled, revealing a yawning spiral chute—an iron serpent twisting downward into suffocating darkness.

His heart hammered. He forced his focus back to Charlotte. With a strangled cry in his throat, he crouched and slid his arms under her limp form. Her head rolled back, a rivulet of blood staining his sleeve; bile rose in his throat, but he swallowed it raw. Inch by inch, he dragged her to the chute's brink. The metallic scent of death sharpened.

A final, frantic heave, and her body tipped over the edge. Flesh met steel with a wet crash, her limbs smacking against the chute's curves like stones tumbling into a well. A sickening crack echoed halfway down—bone against beam—before silence swallowed her.

Ben staggered back, frantically wiping his hands on his trousers. He stared at the splayed book, its weight holding the secret door open. Summoning every ounce of will, he yanked it shut. The door groaned shut, sealing the abyss—and his horror—away.

He bolted from the room, heart pounding like a war drum, the corridor stretching before him in oppressive darkness. One thought pierced the chaos: *leave it open*. Let them think she fell by her own foolish curiosity.

At a grimy window, fingers pressed to the cold glass, he hovered near the back door, cracked open behind him, the night already creeping in. He gazed out into the mist-choked dark. The stars were drowned; the world beyond indifferent, waiting.

~

The first pale fingers of dawn peeled back the inky curtain of night over the sleepy seaside village. A soft, briny breeze drifted in from the

surf, carrying with it the tang of salt and seaweed, and teasing the dew-laden cobblestones
beneath Ben's unhurried steps. Dimly lit windows lay dark and hushed, as though the
whole hamlet held its breath, waiting for the
sun to fully climb the east. Only the harsh,
raucous cries of seagulls shattered the stillness, their wings cleaving through the rosy
sky, casting ragged silhouettes against the
horizon. Ben walked on with an almost buoy-
ant lightness, as if some invisible burden had
slipped free from his shoulders. Above him the
heavens unfurled in a slow gradient of colour-
deep indigo melting into lavender, then blush
pink, then the liquid gold of early morning.
The world felt suspended in this perfect in-be-
tween moment, as though time itself had
paused to offer him one last gift of serenity.
Up above, the seagulls wheeled and cawed in
restless loops, their feathers gleaming silver in
the new light. He watched with a pang of envy.
They were creatures of sky and wind, untethered by regret or responsibility—free to ride
the rising currents, heedless of the wreckage
below. For a heartbeat, Ben closed his eyes
and imagined himself among them: skimming

whitecaps, rising on invisible drafts, weightless above all the choices and mistakes that
had anchored him to this earth.

His fingers itched for something, until they
found the pocket of his coat. There lay the
bloodstained desert rose he had carried like a
silent confession. The crystal-petaled relic
bore the rusty streaks of that violent night—
each jagged edge a reminder of what he could
never unmake. He paused at the cliff-faced
promenade, where the ocean stretched out in
rolling sheets of blue and grey.

Slowly he drew the rose from its hiding place.
The coarse facets bit into his palm, the weight
of it firm and real. With a deliberate flick of
his wrist, he sent it arcing into the morning
tide. It plummeted through the glassy surface,
a sharp splash echoing in the quiet air, then
sank into the depths, carried away by the current's pull.

Behind him the village stirred awake: wooden
shutters clattered open, the scent of fresh
bread wavered from a bakery door, and distant voices rose in that gentle, instinctive hum
of daily life renewing itself. Yet Ben felt removed—an unseen observer behind a glass

pane—watching the world revolve without him. The sun climbed higher, scattering warm amber light across tiled rooftops and cobble work lanes. Its rays kissed his shoulders, but the touch felt hollow, like a memory of warmth he once knew. He drifted from the shore toward the old station at the village's edge, each footstep carrying him farther from the man he had been.

Inside the station platform, the air buzzed faintly with expectation. A handful of bleary-eyed commuters leaned against iron pillars, clutching coffee cups that steamed in the chill. The rails gleamed like polished ribbons, tracing a straight path into the unknown. Ben paused at the platform's edge, hands sunk deep into his coat pockets, gaze locked on the horizon where steel tracks vanished into morning mist.

A distant rumble began to throb beneath his feet. It grew steadily, a low pulse that sharpened into the unmistakable roar of an approaching train. The ground vibrated—wood and steel humming in mournful unison—the distant roar swelling into something ancient, inevitable, and final.

He closed his eyes.

In that brief darkness, he saw what might have been: the release of a burden he had carried for so long without ever learning its name. The thrill of escape beneath a sky that had never truly felt like his. A fleeting promise of redemption waiting on the other side—quiet, tender, and real.

The train's headlights pierced the morning mist like eyes he could not lie to.

A sudden calm settled in his chest. The scent of hot engine oil and scorched metal filled his lungs. His heartbeat quickened. He drew a single breath, slow and deliberate.

Then, with his mind startlingly clear, he leaned forward—and stepped onto the tracks.

2.

ASH

"The worst part of holding the memories is not the pain. It's the loneliness of it." —Lois Lowry

The chill in the air clung to every surface, coating the cemetery in a thin layer of frost that glittered dully beneath the overcast sky. The clouds hung low and leaden, swallowing any hint of sunlight and muting the colours of the world into a palette of pewter and ash. No birds sang. No breeze stirred the skeletal branches overhead. Even the earth felt hard and unyielding—as though the ground itself had stiffened in solemn deference to the gathering. Small, ragged groups of mourners clustered around the freshly dug grave, their breaths blooming like ghostly flowers in the frigid air. Each person was lost in the private resonance of sorrow, a solitary figure in a sea of shared heartbreak.

Among them stood a lone woman, shoulders hunched beneath her wool coat, her face hidden in shadow as she bowed her head. Strands of her golden hair had escaped the morning's tidy bun, shimmering like threads of sunlight against the grey backdrop—and even so she barely seemed aware of them. The wind skated across her cheeks, lifting wisps of hair and trailing them across her pale skin, but she did not move to brush them away. Her hands were thrust deep into her coat pockets, knuckles white around unseen fists, as the priest's ritualistic voice drifted through the stillness. She heard only its distant hum.

Before her rested a coffin, its polished mahogany surface the sole point of warmth in the frozen landscape. The lacquer gleamed dully under the dim sky, reflecting broken shards of light that trembled like tears. It waited upon the lowering straps, poised to slip into the yawning abyss below. The very shape of it— pristine, petite—was a cruel testament to innocence lost, and its presence pressed heavily on every heart there.

She listened to the priest's words of consolation as if through water, distant and distorted, while stifled sobs drifted from behind her like mournful windchimes. All she could see was the gaping rectangle in the ground, the pit carved into the earth to swallow her brother Colin. Once a bright, mischievous boy who had followed her everywhere, he was now nothing more than cold wood and finality. The thought knotted in her chest, squeezing out any warm spark of hope. There was no comfort, no closure—only the inexorable frost of regret.

A few paces away, their mother stood as though sculpted from marble: her posture rigid, chin lifted, her eyes concealed by oversized black sunglasses that mirrored the pale sky. Even in grief, she seemed determined to project perfection—the tailored lines of her coat nipped tightly at the waist, the silk scarf knotted with precision. Mourning was merely another stage on which to craft an elegant performance. Not far from her, their father lurked on the periphery, hands jammed into coat pockets as if he feared they might slip into some emotional abyss if he released them. He did not cry. He did not speak. He observed with a distant, blank stare, as though the funeral were someone else's and the departed child only a name on a plaque. He had always retreated into pubs and fleeting pleasures, leaving the hard work of family to fall elsewhere—and even now, at his son's burial, he remained disengaged, an actor who had missed his cue.

So they stood: a family bound by blood yet divided by the cold walls each had erected around their heart. Not one voice broke the hush as the priest's incantation wound its way through the rows of tombstones. His words fell like soft snowflakes—gentle, white, ephemeral—only to melt upon contact with the frozen ground of their souls. Grief had long since carved its channels between them, channels no funeral rite could ever refill.
At last, the woman nearest the coffin shifted, as though gathering the courage to step away. Instead, she edged forward, every breath a visible puff of vapor. Her gloved fingers reached out and brushed the lacquered wood. A tremor ran through her, and for the first time since she'd arrived, her inhalation caught like a bird's frantic wingbeat. Her eyes—hollow, rimmed with dryness—focused on the

engraved nameplate: "Colin Petersen," her little brother.

Charlotte stared at the coffin's polished mahogany, the weight of grief pressing on her like the earth soon to cover her brother. A cold wind rustled dead leaves, and she let the priest's droning words fade as she remembered Colin—not the silent figure before her, but the bright-eyed boy who darted through their garden hedges, laughter echoing as he waited to be found in their endless hide-and-seek games, his small hand always reaching for hers.

Her mother stepped closer, the rustle of tailored wool brushing the silence.

"You should've called him back," she murmured—quiet, but cutting. Charlotte didn't turn. Her throat tightened.

"You ignored the school's messages," she replied, voice low, trembling with fury. No answer—just the faint clink of pearls shifting at her mother's neck.

But life's momentum had pulled them apart. She'd been swept into her mother's world of cameras and applause, each shutter clicks demanding a brighter smile, a taller pose, a faster loss of innocence. She recalled the first photoshoot: age six, golden curls catching the spring sun, standing rigid as her mother coached her every tilt and smile. The photographer crouched like a hunter. "Perfect," he whispered, and her mother's grip on her shoulder reminded her to stay still, to perform. In that moment she'd glimpsed her future—shimmering spotlights, endless praise, a promise of something beyond their small realities.

Her mother had seen that single photograph as a fortune to be seized. While their home sagged under utility bills and her father drowned his troubles in pubs, she had invested every ounce of hope in Charlotte's budding promise. She dragged her daughter from one audition to the next, each glossy portfolio another stone in the house she was determined to build—a house of celebrity, designer gowns, and open-bar galas.

At sixteen, the world beyond the agency beckoned in the form of Sven Lindström—a model with cheekbones carved by Michelangelo and a look of amused superiority permanently etched across his face. Their first dinner was at La Belle Époque, a restaurant draped in rose-gold light. Crystal chandeliers hung like frozen waterfalls, refracting candlelight into dancing prisms on polished marble. The aroma of rosemary and truffle oil wove through the air, while silverware lay in precise formation like soldiers at attention. Charlotte stepped in wearing an ivory dress pinned with delicate pearls, each bead an itch against her skin; her mother sat nearby, her own gown a constellation of rhinestones, her hair spun so tight it gleamed like a helmet.

Sven leaned back in his chair, fine wine swirling in his crystal glass. His voice, smooth with a practiced Swedish accent, cut through the quiet clink of cutlery. "They say I look like I stepped out of a Renaissance painting," he declared, as though awaiting thunderous applause. Charlotte forced a smile so brittle it might have cracked. "Yes," she managed, her throat constricting around the word.

He carried on, unperturbed by her reticence, cataloguing his triumphs: campaigns with heritage brands, exclusive shoots in Côte d'Azur villas, a diet consisting solely of Swiss-Alpine spring water. He sneered at other models, labelling them *inferior*, as if the world were divided into his inner circle and everyone else. His gaze raked over Charlotte as though she were a new article of couture.

From across the room, her mother sipped Champagne, her eyes alight with anticipation. She mistook Charlotte's silence for poise, interpreted the tension in her daughter's shoulders as demure charm. Each approving nod only tightened the invisible noose of expectation around Charlotte's spirit.

Then, with a fluid flourish, Sven described his yacht—Eden, he called it—a floating palace where the jet set danced beneath riggings of fairy lights. "You must join me," he insisted, inclining his head in invitation. His casual grin set Charlotte's stomach roiling.

Later, when her mother inquired after the evening, Charlotte rehearsed her reply as meticulously as she had rehearsed every pose. "It was delightful," she said, her tone even, her expression smooth as porcelain. Her mother clasped her hands and beamed, already drafting plans for tomorrow's tête-à-tête. And so, the courtship continued. Chopin sonatas of bragging filled each dinner; she nodded and smiled, the dutiful accessory on his arm. He never asked about her passions, her dreams, the faint flicker of fear in her heart. In his world she existed solely as spectacle—an exquisite prop in his personal pageant. The realization hollowed her, as though she were a mannequin in a shop window, dressed for someone else's delight.

Charlotte had been everything her mother once longed to be—a child star with a perfect smile plastered across magazine covers, a fixture on glossy billboards. While other girls her age rode bicycles or chased laughter through playgrounds, she had learned to angle her chin, arch her back, and hold the camera's gaze with unerring precision. She was told she was special, destined for greatness outside the narrow streets of suburbia—and she believed it, for her mother believed it too.

Even beneath the glare of a thousand stage lights and the relentless staccato of camera flashes, Colin had always existed at the very edge of perception—so faint that he might have been a trick of the light or a shadow slipping across the wall. His presence was quieter than the low hum of the projector in the screening room, smaller than a whisper shared in the hush between scenes, almost impossible to see unless you paused and truly searched. He was the boy who melted into the ornate wallpaper patterns at home—his shape dissolving into swirls of cream and gold—leaving behind only the faintest echo, a residue of breath and unspoken words. While Charlotte dazzled in sequins and chiffon beneath spotlights, his figure receded into a gentle, muted haze, as though someone had turned down the dimmer on his brightness. It wasn't that Charlotte lacked love for him—she treasured him in her own way—but her life had long since become a whirlwind of fittings, last-minute photo shoots in distant cities, and rehearsed red carpet smiles. She had never paused long enough to really see Colin, to discern the ache behind his downcast eyes or the way his shoulders curved inward, year after year, like an old book slowly losing its spine.

Now, as she knelt beside his fresh mound of earth, a terrible clarity struck her like icy rain. The scent of chrysanthemums—pure white and trembling in the cold air—mingled with the damp, loamy perfume of freshly turned soil. Every inhalation felt like a confession: the dirt, the chill, the humid weight of regret pressing against her lungs. The stiff wind tugged at the delicate lace at her throat and caught the edges of her mourning veil, whipping it into a brief flutter before settling it back into place.

In that moment, she realized she had failed him—her brother, her blood—and that everyone around them had done the same.

Her thoughts wandered back to the warning signs she had overlooked, like forgotten pages in a book. She recalled Colin quietly moving down the hallway to his room, his hand brushing the doorknob before it clicked shut, locking her out as if he wished to keep his pain hidden forever. She remembered the school reports arriving in envelopes stamped with red ink, each filled with phrases like *withdrawn, reluctant to engage,* and *"struggling to participate,* as if his name had become just an entry in an academic record. She envisioned him at the dinner table, his meal untouched, his eyes tracing the faded floral pattern on the tablecloth instead of meeting hers. Charlotte, caught up in chasing the next campaign and perfecting her runway walk, was too engrossed in her own goals to notice her brother's deteriorating spirit.

Margaret Petersen was the epitome of contrasting faces: pristine in custom-tailored designer suits, her lipstick always applied with such precision it looked as though an artist had used a stencil. To the cameras, she was the devoted matriarch, beaming at her daughter with a warmth that lit every flashbulb. Yet the moment the lenses blinked off; she withdrew behind a wall of cool reserve. Charlotte learned early on that her mother's affection was a performance—a scripted gesture reserved for public appearances, a bit of stage fog that dispersed the instant the footlights dimmed. Their father was a different kind of shadow—a man who drifted in and out of their lives like smoke curling from an extinguished candle. His broad shoulders, once as steady as oak beams, had bowed under years of quiet disappointments. He came home just long enough to deposit a pay check on the hall table and then vanished into the amber glow of his favourite pub, leaving behind the tang of whisky on his breath and an unpaid bar tab that told its own story of absence. He had no patience for Hollywood glamor, or the meticulous façades Margaret maintained. Neither of his children ever truly captured his devotion; Colin, ever the silent one, barely registered on his radar at all.

For Colin, the fractured household was a minefield. He expertly sidestepped conflicts, slipping into corners where he could become nearly invisible. His voice dwindled to a whisper, rarely heard by anyone. He mastered the art of fading away like a loose thread disappearing into a seam. As his cheeks lost colour, ribs showed through his t-shirts, and hands trembled with hidden anguish, no one noticed—not his perfectly made up mother, his silently bitter father, nor Charlotte, always chasing the spotlight, believing that the rumours of slipping grades were nothing more than background noise, that the faint bruises on his forearms were the clumsiness of a boy his age. Her world was an incandescent blur that left no space to feel or observe another soul's sorrow.

Standing at his graveside now, she watched Margaret arrange her tailored mourning dress with clinical precision, securing each fold as though designing a new runway ensemble rather than dressing for loss. Her mother's black-rimmed sunglasses were like opaque shields, hiding an unreadable expression. Even her tears seemed rehearsed, glistening for the benefit of onlookers rather than flowing from genuine grief.

If Margaret's love had been a commodity doled out only when Charlotte's career soared, their father's love had been a ghost—always promised, never delivered. He never kissed foreheads or tucked either child in at night. His idea of discipline was the echo of his boots on the stairs as he departed floor by floor, night after night. To Charlotte, his indifference had felt like a thousand little cuts. And Colin? He had no chance at all against such neglect.

Their marriage had begun like so many others—a collision of youthful optimism and naive promises made in the warm glow of early affection. Two people married too young, their vows exchanged in the naive belief that love alone could bridge the vast distances between their private fears and unspoken dreams. They had clung to each other in those early years, Margaret rehearsing her role as the devoted wife, her husband playing the part of the steadfast provider. But as the years passed, they had grown apart in the silence of their shared rooms. Margaret fulfilled her role as wife and mother with the precision of a seasoned actress, her every gesture a small act of defiance against the crumbling facade of their marriage. Her husband, meanwhile, had retreated into his own shadows, his affections slowly withdrawing like the tide, leaving behind a barren stretch of emotional distance. He had become a ghost within his own home, his presence marked only by the faint trace of aftershave in the hallway and the low creak of the front door as he left, yet again, for another long night out.

This slow decay of their marriage had shaped Charlotte's perception of love, warping it into something fragile and transactional. She learned early that affection came with strings attached, that a single misstep could shatter the fragile peace of their home. Her mother's rancour became a force she could neither

escape nor placate, and her father's indifference taught her that love could be withdrawn
without warning, that silence could be more
painful than words, that the absence of affection could cut deeper than any harsh rebuke.

After the funeral, Charlotte found herself
caught in a muted haze of black tie acquaint-
ances murmuring condolences and bouquets
of perfume-soaked condolence cards stacked
in an ever-growing pile. She retreated behind
curt phone messages to agents and stylists,
shutting them out as if they, too, might betray
her if she let them in. The couture gowns, the
limousines, the glittering frenzy of her former
life suddenly felt suffocating, shallow, devoid
of any genuine purpose. What had all her
beauty and success ever protected? Not her
brother.

For the first time in her life, she questioned
every choice she had ever made. Who was she
beneath the layer of makeup and the armour
of designer labels? What value did her reflection hold if it couldn't shield the one person
who had always needed her most? And in that
questioning, a seed of resolve took root. She
would walk away from the only world she had

ever known—the world that had built her up and imprisoned her at once—and she would seek something more real, something that mattered beyond the angle of her jaw or the curve of her silhouette. She told Margaret she planned to quit the industry. Her mother's reaction was like the sudden crack of thunder: rage flaring behind those flawlessly arched eyebrows. "You can't just throw your life away," she hissed, her voice trembling with false outrage. "All those contracts, and the money—don't you understand what this means?" But Charlotte felt no tremor of doubt. That night, after her parents left with their tin of lemon bars and hollow smiles, Charlotte hurled a vase across the kitchen. It shattered, water and daisies scattering across the tile. She sank to the floor, dress soaking through, and let the sobs rip her open.

For the first time in her life, she was acting solely for herself.

With every modelling contract she declined, every glossy magazine cover she let slip through her fingers, a tangible weight lifted from her chest. She packed away the tulle and silk gowns, locked them in trunks at the back of her closet, and turned down invitations that once would have been the pinnacle of her existence.

~

In the days after the funeral, the house itself seemed to breathe differently, as if it were finally exhaling years of tightly coiled tension. The silence was almost unbearable—a cavern where Colin's presence had once been palpable. Charlotte drifted through the rooms like a sleepwalker, weighed down by a heaviness that clung to every surface. Her mother's footsteps grew lighter, more hesitant, and her father's presence receded into an even fainter shadow. The walls felt colder, as though frost had sneaked in and settled into the marrow of their lives. After Colin's death, they never spoke of him. Charlotte remembered the silence more than any grief. Her mother filled the calendar with new auditions. Her father called it 'focus.' No one asked how she slept. No one asked if she ate. She became their surviving miracle and surviving meant performance.

Haunted by his death and by the realization that her world had been too small, too absorbed in her own ambitions to notice his quiet suffering, Charlotte found herself unable to return to her former life. She lacked the strength to slip into gowns or pose for glossy shoots; the thought of facing the camera again left her feeling exposed in a way she'd never known. It wasn't just the public she dreaded— it was herself. She'd never been so estranged from her own reflection.

Her mother insisted, "You have to keep working, Charlotte." But Charlotte only stared at her pale face in the hallway mirror and felt, with startling clarity, that she could no longer perform. Colin's death had cleaved her life into before and after, and no amount of stitching could make her whole again.

One evening, she found herself in Colin's room, perched on his bed and clutching his worn sketchbook. His drawings were simple—

endless seas with ships, lofty mountains shrouded in mist—until she turned to a page showing a lone figure atop a hill, arms wrapped around itself under a raging storm, a bare tree bowed beside it. The image burrowed into her heart like a vine, and she almost heard Colin's soft, tentative voice reading aloud to himself. He had always felt alone, even in a crowd, and she had been too engrossed in her own life to see it.

Guilt swelled inside her, but alongside it flickered something else: responsibility, purpose. She couldn't undo her brother's suicide, nor could she bring him back, but she could alter the path ahead. Colin's death didn't have to mark an end—it could spark something meaningful.

The next day, she was at the library, hunting for answers. She pulled books on grief, psychology, mental health programs for isolated youth, articles on suicide prevention and trauma intervention. That night, long after her parents' lights were out, she spread printouts and textbooks across the dining table and opened her laptop to a university's course catalogue. Child Psychology. Trauma Studies.

Mental Health Counselling. For the first time in years, a fierce determination lit inside her. Abandoning her old life and the expectations that had shaped her felt daunting, but it was no longer just about her. It was about honouring Colin's memory and ensuring that no one else would feel as invisible. She set about her university applications, pouring over dog-eared catalogues and margin—scrawled notes deep into the quiet hours. With each syllabus she studied, a new sense of purpose dawned—gentle but unstoppable, like first light breaking over the horizon.

Then, on a humid midsummer morning, an acceptance letter arrived. She held it in trembling hands as though it were a guiding beacon, promising fulfilment not through the brilliance of flashbulb smiles but through the profound silence of empathy.

She was twenty-two upon her arrival at the university campus. The memory of Colin's funeral still etched in the edges of her vision, though two years had passed, the world of stylists and paparazzi faded into the background, replaced by the distinctive scent of chalk dust and the nostalgic perfume of aged books. The air was filled with the low hum of lecterns and the vibrant debates that reverberated through the lecture halls. Initially, she felt like an imposter, donning carefully chosen knit sweaters and clutching borrowed textbooks, but, as she settled into this new academic life, she discovered a surprising advantage rooted in her past experiences.

~

During her second year of postgraduate studies, Charlotte felt as though she were running a race she could never win—and yet, with every paper accepted and every seminar she led, she inched ever closer to the front of the pack. By then, the relentless pace of academic life had become her normal: early mornings spent poring over journals in the flickering lights of the library, afternoons punctuated by impromptu debates with professors, evenings lost in the glow of her laptop as she drafted proposals and dissected theories. She'd climbed to the top of her cohort, earned the respect of peers and mentors alike, but deep inside, she carried a hollow emptiness—a quiet ache that no grant award or glowing recommendation could ever fill.

In that moment, when the exhilaration of success was tinged with the subtle ache of solitude, Charlotte noticed Thomas for the very first time. Their paths crossed in a rather plain seminar room, tucked away just off the main corridor dedicated to the humanities. The room was filled with rows of folding chairs and a chalkboard that bore remnants of someone else's scribbled notes. Thomas was seated near the back, distinctly apart from the crowd of other graduate students who were all vying for the professor's attention with an air of brashness, but he didn't partake in their antics. Instead, he exuded an aura of serene composure, his hands neatly folded on the desk, his head inclined slightly to one side, as if he were attuned not to the droning voice of the lecturer but to an ethereal melody that only he could discern. As Charlotte lifted her gaze from the notes she was meticulously taking, her eyes met his, and in that brief exchange, a spark ignited—a silent acknowledgment passed between them. It was as if they both understood the relentless pursuit of a dream that always seemed just out of reach.

Over the ensuing weeks, Charlotte gradually unravelled the layers of Thomas's tranquil demeanour, discovering that it was deeply rooted in a childhood she could only envision in her wildest dreams. He had been nurtured by two devoted parents who had gently guided him through every challenge life presented, always offering quiet encouragement. They had been present at every school recital, every science fair, and every family dinner, their presence unwavering and free of any trace of resentment or regret. When Thomas spoke of them, his face would light up with a warmth so genuine that it captivated Charlotte, drawing her closer to him time and time again. She found herself longing for even a small measure of the security he seemed to take for granted, a security she had never known but deeply yearned for.

Their first real conversation unfolded almost by chance—Charlotte hurrying out of the lecture hall, her laptop bag swaying precariously from one shoulder, and Thomas casually matching her stride. What initially started as a straightforward discussion about that afternoon's talk on narrative theory gradually eased into more intimate matters: the relentless pressure of dissertation research, the countless sleepless nights spent in pursuit of credits, the fears they both held about whether their relentless efforts would ever truly measure up. Before Charlotte realized it, she was revealing memories she had kept locked away—those childhood summers spent trying to escape her parents' volatile arguments, the secret shame she still bore about Colin, the friend she had hurt, and the guilt that lurked like a shadow.

What grew between them wasn't the intense, all-consuming passion that Charlotte had always associated with love—the tumultuous, firework-filled romances that flared brightly and extinguished just as quickly. Instead, it was something more subtle, almost unnoticed at first: a gentle warmth that nestled in her chest like embers after a fire had burned out, a quiet comfort that replaced her usual restlessness. Thomas didn't overwhelm her with grand proclamations; he didn't sweep her off her feet with dramatic gestures. He simply appeared—reliably, without fanfare—offering the rare gift of consistency.

As days grew into weeks, their study sessions stretched into late night café conversations over steaming mugs of dark roast. They argued playfully over interpretations of literary texts, compared notes on research methods, and then gradually slipped into more intimate exchanges hopes for the future, regrets from the past, confessions whispered in the soft hum of fluorescent lights. When Charlotte's voice cracked as she revisited her remorse over Colin, Thomas didn't flinch or offer meaningless reassurances. He just listened—eyes steady, expression open—until she could find her own way to breathe again. Charlotte, who had spent so long hiding behind a mask of perfection in a world that demanded brilliance at every turn, found this unguarded acceptance at once exhilarating and terrifying. To be seen without artifice, to let someone witness her flaws and remain steadfast—she realized this was freedom she had never allowed herself to taste. But beneath the sweetness of relief, a small current of anxiety began to stir: what if this calm could vanish as quickly as it had come? What if she were merely projecting onto him the stability she craved, only to be disappointed?

Over the course of the following months, their friendship blossomed in ways Charlotte could never have foreseen. She first sensed it as a gentle flutter of anticipation, a subtle thrill, before one of their leisurely walks home. It was when Thomas, with his steady presence, reached out to support her while they carefully navigated the uneven and cracked sidewalk. It was in the gentle warmth that spread through her whenever he lingered a moment too long in conversation, their hands accidentally brushing against each other on the shared bench at the quad, creating an electric charge that lingered in the air. Despite her determined efforts to smother her burgeoning affection beneath stacks of reading assignments and looming deadlines, her thoughts persistently wandered back to the steady contours of his face and the quiet sincerity that resonated in his voice.

Charlotte repeatedly told herself—rationally, sternly—that there was no space for romance amid the whirlwind of university reports, presentations, and the planning of her future career. She reminded herself that she had witnessed far too many brilliant connections burn out under the weight of expectations and unfulfilled promises. Yet, each morning, she found a fresh cup of jasmine tea waiting on her desk—a thoughtful gesture that spoke volumes. Every afternoon, Thomas would gracefully slide into the empty seat beside her during lectures, his presence becoming as natural and essential as breathing. With each small, thoughtful gesture, the magnetic pull between them grew stronger, intricately weaving itself into the very fabric of her days and nights.

Then, on one crisp autumn evening after an exhaustive marathon study session, the shift that had been quietly simmering beneath the surface finally crystallized into something tangible.
The campus was bathed in a warm glow of gold and shadow, the lampposts flickering to life as twilight gently descended. Thomas graciously offered to walk her back to her dorm,

as had become their comforting routine, and this time, neither of them spoke—words felt intrusive amidst the serene hush of falling leaves and the faint echo of distant laughter from student gatherings. As they paused at her doorway, Charlotte's heart pounded so loudly within her chest that she was certain he could hear its frantic beat, marking the undeniable turning point in their entwined journey. "I really enjoyed tonight," he murmured, his voice low, almost hesitant.

"Me too," she breathed, struggling to keep her tone steady as warmth flooded her cheeks.

He searched her eyes in that moment, and she recognized the same mixture of hope and fear that had come to define her own feelings.

Then, as unobtrusively as a thought, he leaned in and brushed his lips to hers. There were no fireworks, no cinematic crescendo—just a soft, tender promise that felt more electrifying than any grand display she'd ever known. It wasn't an ending; it was an invitation to begin something new. When they finally pulled away, speechless, Charlotte realized that at last the void inside her had softened, if not vanished outright, replaced by something gentler and infinitely more sustaining than any empty triumph she'd ever chased.

~

In the weeks that followed, Charlotte and Thomas slipped into a shared cadence so unhurried it might have been measured in sighs rather than seconds. There was no whirlwind of dizzy courtship—no dawn-lit phone calls, no frantic love letters pressed into trembling hands. Instead, their companionship unfurled like tendrils of ivy creeping up a stone wall, each new leaf of connection revealing itself in its own good time. Every evening, as the golden hour surrendered to twilight, Thomas would shoulder his weathered backpack and step into the hush of the campus library. Charlotte would be there before him, already unpacking her journals, her pens arranged in a neat fan across the polished oak. A faint trace of her lavender lotion lingered in the air, mingling with the old-book musk that drifted between the stacks. She'd glance up, offer him a small smile, and settle in. Under the pale glow of the desk lamp, they tackled problem sets and underlined complicated passages, voices low enough to keep their conversation cocooned within their own little world. Minutes blended into hours, the lamp's glow softening as they worked side by side, turning pages in silent synchronicity.

Every so often, Charlotte's elbow would brush his, or their notebooks would gently overlap, forcing them to scoot closer. In those tiny collisions she discovered a new sort of ease—the tender warmth where his forearm pressed against hers, the shy caress of his thigh as they leaned toward the same line of text. Her breath would catch for a heartbeat, a small thrill that felt as familiar as the rise and fall of the tide. It was as if two puzzle pieces designed to fit together were at last clicking into place, without spectacle or applause.

~

As time slipped by, that gentle familiarity morphed into something almost too quiet, a rhythm that now lacked any crescendo. Those once thrilling, electric touches faded into the predictability of shared routines. She was torn between appreciating the calm and yearning for the chaos that used to make her heart race. It was a slow-growing disquiet, the kind that festers in the shadows of unexamined satisfaction. The warmth she had cherished now felt like a burden, a steady pulse where she craved a sudden spark. She confused the absence of conflict with the absence of passion, unable to recognize that in those silent moments—elbows brushing, thighs touching, notebooks overlapping—was the quiet promise of a lasting bond. It was a connection not rooted in fevered intensity but in the trust of two lives intentionally interwoven. She couldn't shake the feeling of something missing, caught in her internal battle between longing for the past's fire and the present's steady embrace.

One evening, when the stacks beyond their desk dissolved into shadow, the lamp's amber light pooled around them like honey. All Charlotte could see was Thomas's profile: the shadowed sweep of his lashes, the gentle slope of his nose, the steady rhythm of his chest. He set his pen down, hands hovering as though he'd paused mid-thought. Then, slowly, almost reverently, he reached across the table and tucked a loose strand of her hair behind her ear. "Are you all right?" he whispered, his voice so soft it could have been the rustle of leaves in a breeze—a private question meant only for her. Charlotte felt her heart drumming against her ribcage, loud enough that she worried he might hear it. She swallowed, lacing her fingers around his knuckles. "I'm... I'm fine," she managed, her voice trembling with the echo of her own relief. She realized, in that moment, that she no longer felt the twinge of self-consciousness that used to knot in her stomach when someone watched her too closely. Thomas had a way of making her feel seen and safe all at once. He offered her a gentle tilt of his head, as though asking permission, and when she nodded, he leaned in with a deliberation that slowed time itself. The world contracted to the curve of her lips, the faint scent of his shirt, the press of his palm against the small of her back. His kiss was soft, unhurried—a slow bloom of warmth that spoke more of trust than of reckless desire. His fingers threaded through hers, conveying wordlessly, *I'm here. Take all the time you need.*

Afterward, they lingered in the hush of the library, hearts echoing the shared rhythm of that kiss.

When at last they gathered their things, marking the end of one reverie and the beginning of the next, their footsteps echoed down the narrow corridor. Thomas guided her to a quiet study room nestled between ancient stone walls. The single bed there was draped in a thick woven spread, its muted pattern reminiscent of autumn leaves. The air smelled faintly of lavender soap and old cotton, and in the low light, the room felt like a sacred hiding place.

He gently helped her onto the bed with the same delicate care one might use when placing a fragile bird into its nest, supporting her

DEAR READER

YOU'VE JUST STUMBLED UPON A GIFT.

THIS ISN'T JUST A BOOK—IT'S A PIECE OF MY HEART, LEFT QUIETLY IN THE WORLD FOR A STRANGER TO FIND. IT'S A STORY I NEEDED TO WRITE. A STORY THAT MIGHT, IN SOME SMALL WAY, FIND A PLACE IN YOU TOO.

IF IT STAYS WITH YOU, I WOULD BE GRATEFUL BEYOND WORDS TO HEAR FROM YOU. YOU CAN LEAVE A SHORT REVIEW OR POST A PHOTO USING THE QR CODES BELOW, OR SHARE IT ON INSTAGRAM WITH: **#FORALLTHETIMESBOOK** OR **#BOOKSINTHEWILD**

AND WHEN THE FINAL PAGE TURNS, DON'T KEEP IT TO YOURSELF. PASS IT ON. LEAVE IT SOMEWHERE UNEXPECTED. LET IT WHISPER TO THE NEXT READER.

LET'S SEE HOW FAR A STORY CAN TRAVEL.

Thank you

shoulders to ensure she wouldn't fall. Yet, there lingered a tension she could not ignore—an internal tug of war between longing and fear. There was no urgency, no blaring lights, no hurried sense of obligation like on the runway, no hidden disrespect, objectification, or unwanted touching. But she couldn't shake the feeling of being trapped by her own desires. In the soft dimness of the room, Charlotte began to wonder if this was what she had been missing with Thomas—a trace of aggression she thought she had escaped, the scars of which should not bind her, though she now felt an unsettling yearning to be: bound.

Charlotte let out a long, quiet sigh, her mind torn as her body began to unfurl, every muscle relaxing as though she had been holding her breath for days. Thomas stayed close, his hands softly gliding over her back with a reverence that made her feel cherished. Each touch was an unspoken promise—that he would handle her heart with the same tenderness as he did her skin, but her heart whispered doubts she couldn't quite silence.

Their lovemaking was not a hurried frenzy but a gradual unfolding of breath and warmth, a gentle dance of lips and whispered names. Was this what she desired? Or did she long to be overwhelmed into submission instead? The wind tapped softly at the windowpanes, providing a gentle rhythm, but within, they moved with a relaxed harmony, as if guided by the soothing sound of distant waves. Barely conscious of where one body ended and the other began, Charlotte immersed herself in the softness of his touch, in the comforting pressure of his chest against hers. As their fervour faded to a gentle glow, they lay intertwined, Thomas's arm resting across her waist, the steady beat of his heart beneath her ear like a vow: *you are safe here.*

"Do you feel all right?" he murmured into the hush.

Charlotte nestled her cheek against the comforting warmth of his chest, her fingers delicately tracing the ridges of his collarbone.

"Mm—hmm," she murmured softly, though inside, a small, cold knot of worry twisted in her stomach.

Was this tenderness truly enough for her? Had she confused gentleness with love, and quiet devotion with passion? What if, beneath it all, she still longed for the sharp edges, the way desire once felt like a challenge she needed to conquer? She wondered if this serenity was merely an illusion, one that would shatter when the novelty wore off, revealing her true self—a woman who had been desired, used, and discarded. Would he eventually yearn for the spark she no longer knew how to ignite? Her heart was torn, caught between the comfort of now and the haunting echoes of what once was.

Long after Thomas had fallen asleep, Charlotte remained awake, observing the fragmented moonlight dancing across the ceiling. Her fingers traced the faint scar on her palm as she replayed the moments of their closeness, searching for any sign of doubt in his eyes or any indication that his tenderness was merely an act. She tried to assure herself that this was enough—his steady breath beside her, his hand warm against her hip, should have been sufficient.

The silence disturbed her. The absence of urgent whispers and desperate embraces, the calm that should have been comforting, only left her feeling empty. What if, once the excitement of their routine wore off, his touch became an obligation instead of a desire? What if their love, lacking conflict, became something insubstantial and easily discarded? She recalled the backstage chaos of her past life—the hands that grabbed her without permission, the eyes that assessed her worth based on her appearance, the rapid commands of photographers who saw her as nothing more than a mannequin adorned in silk. It had been degrading, though also thrilling in a way she couldn't completely dismiss. In that world, she knew her value, even if it was a harsh, transactional one.

Now, lying in the darkness next to a man who treated her skin with reverence, she wondered if she had exchanged high stakes chaos for a quieter confinement—a life where her fears spoke louder than her lover's reassurances. Would he still view her the same way when he realized her scars went deeper than the thin line on her palm?

~

In the days that unfolded after the initial stirrings of her anxiety, she found her worries weaving themselves intricately into the fabric of her everyday life, leaving her feeling conflicted and disoriented. When Thomas's text messages arrived later than she had come to expect, she became consumed with the urge to check her phone repeatedly, her eyes stinging with the exhaustion of too many sleepless nights, yet she remained incapable of tearing her gaze away from the screen. She was trapped in an endless loop of anticipation and dread. If Thomas cancelled a study date—even when he provided the most logical and reasonable explanation—she found herself slipping into a disquieting silence. Her mind waged a war between the rational understanding of his reasons and the pervasive fear that this was an indication of an emotional distance growing between them. During lectures, she became hyperaware, obsessively measuring the distance between their desks, her mind meticulously noting every minuscule shift in his

posture. She struggled intensely with the internal debate over whether these changes were merely coincidental or if they were a silent, unspoken judgment on her self-worth, leaving her trapped in a cycle of doubt and insecurity. Thomas met her unsettled moods with patience. He left small bouquets of daisies—her favourite—in a glass jar at her doorstep, the bright petals defying the grey of her morning. Her inbox overflowed with gentle messages: "Thinking of you," "Hope your day is going well," "Can't wait to see you tonight."
He held her hand when her eyes flickered with doubt, ran his fingers through her hair when she sighed, but she found that no gesture could erase the ache left by years of expecting love to vanish. She thought back to the childhood applause she'd been trained to crave. Love, she had learned, was something earned by performance—and just as swiftly withdrawn the moment she faltered.

For a precious stretch of days, she let herself believe in something steadier. Weekends were spent wandering sunlit streets, sharing crispy tacos from a food truck parked beneath a canopy of maples. They paused on a stone bridge to watch the river swirl, fingers brushing as they reached for the same railing. Back in Charlotte's cramped kitchen, they made risotto together: the soft pop of Arborio rice against the pan, the scent of onion sweetening the air, steam fogging the window as Charlotte performed a dramatic flourish of grated Parmesan—half of it tumbling onto the floor. Thomas laughed, scooped up the stray shreds, and pressed a kiss to her temple before returning them to the pot. In those golden hours, her old anxieties loosened their grip, and she dared to feel something like belonging.

But the sense of peace never lasted.

Each joyful moment was shadowed by the fear: what if he grew weary of calming her doubts? What if, someday, his gentle nature faded away like dew in the morning sun? Why was he always so patient? Why didn't he fight for their relationship? What if the spark had truly disappeared for good?

Her pleas for reassurance grew more desperate. "Do you really love me?" she'd ask, her voice strained. If he hurried downstairs for coffee—her almond milk latte noted on a Post-it—she'd confront him at the door with the

cup, immediately pointing out, "See? You did-
n't even think to ask for the almond milk."
Thomas would pause mid-step, a flicker of
weariness in his eyes, before he softened into
that patient smile of his. He'd ruffle her hair,
shrug, and murmur, "I'm trying, I promise,"
but her doubts clung like winter chill to her
bones. Each apology from him felt like a plaster over a wound that ran far deeper than a
missed latte order.

Throughout this time, Charlotte's mind replayed her past experiences: the bright stages
where she stood under the intense spotlight,
receiving applause for her talent, only to have
her mistakes highlighted in harsh headlines
the next day. She recalled the admirers who
were drawn to her promising youth—not seeking a true woman, but the idea of one. They
were captivated by the perfect smile, the
graceful walk down a runway, a fantasy of
womanhood that existed only in their imagi-
nations. To them, she was not truly a person,
but more of a blank canvas, an outline for
their dreams—a body to adorn, a face to show-
case, a silence to fill with their desires. They
loved her polished image but turned away at

any sign of the real, flawed woman underneath.

For them, a woman's value was temporary, determined by measurements, angles, and the sway of her hips—a collection of traits defined by male expectations. She was seen as the promise of desire without the weight of depth, a symbol of purity without the complexity of identity. Whenever she strayed from that illusion, showed her fears, or slipped from perfection, she felt their interest fade, their eyes grow distant, and their touch withdraw, as if her humanity was a nuisance.

Amidst the chaos of their expectations and her own reflection, she lost her sense of self. She struggled to find her true identity beneath the layers of performance, unable to reconcile the living, breathing person with the polished figure they once admired and then abandoned. She remembered the empty sound of her parents' chairs scraping away from the kitchen table, and the vacant seat where her brother should have been. Love, she thought, wasn't something that left—it simply failed to stay. Nevertheless, there were moments when she allowed the possibility of something different.

Each sunrise found them side by side in the library, hands brushing in familiar greeting, each twilight, their gazes meeting in unspoken conversation. Even as her chest tightened with dread, she chose, again and again, to lean into Thomas's steady presence. And in the gentle pauses between heartbeats, she caught sight of a new truth: that love might not have to collapse under the weight of her past, that maybe—just maybe—it could endure, held secure by countless small, imperfect attempts to stay. So, they continued, imperfectly intertwined: two souls learning to trust the slow music of a love that refused to be hurried, a love that whispered, every day, in the softest of cadences, *I'm not going anywhere.*

~

Their love advanced at a glacial pace, each small step taken with the utmost warp of caution, as though they were balancing on a threadbare silk ribbon stretched taut above a yawning chasm. Dawn came as a gentle intruder each morning, peeling back the covers of night and revealing their fragile connection anew. Charlotte would slip across the threshold of Thomas's apartment before the sun could claim the sky, her feet bare or clad in soft slippers that muted her steps against the worn hardwood floor. The air was always cool, carrying the distant flicker of streetlights. She moved with an almost reverent hush, as if fear of startling him kept her breath shallow. In her hands she bore two ceramic mugs, their surfaces splotched and uneven from years of repeated use. The chipped rim of one told stories of careless knocks against tile and the steady erosion of time. She placed them side by side on the narrow counter, her fingertips grazing the porcelain in a tender, anxious caress. Her pulse shifted in her throat as she reached for the coffee pot, lifting its lid in a small ceremony. The dark liquid poured out in a steady rivulet, steam spiralling upward in lazy corkscrews that fogged the small kitchen window. The scent was rich and bitter, a

145

fragrance that settled into Thomas's shirt with intimate familiarity. He materialized at her elbow just as she was filling the second mug, offering a soft grunt of gratitude that felt like a prayer answered. His hands closed around the warmth; fingers splayed over the ceramic as though it anchored him to something real. In the pale wash of early light, his profile softened: the gentle slope of his brow, the way his lashes cast slender shadows on his cheek. In that moment, Charlotte's heart both soared with relief—relief that they were here, together—and contracted with a prick of guilt, as if she leaned too heavily on this routine, too wholly on him for her sense of stability.

A few weeks prior, they had confidently walked side by side into Hayfield Health Centre, fresh graduates eager to take on new responsibilities. Thanks to Charlotte's convincing efforts in getting their course director to write a persuasive referral letter, they were both offered positions there. They found a modest but practical apartment nearby; Charlotte chose the decor and most of the furnishings, and Thomas allowed her to express her creative flair.

At work, Charlotte paused before Thomas's door, watching through thin strips of frosted glass as he bent over a stack of patient charts, the soft click-click of his pen like a metronome. Drawing a breath, she laid her palm against the cool metal of the handle, then offered him a wavering wave when he looked up. The crinkle at the corners of his eyes sparked like sunrise behind winter clouds, and for a moment Charlotte felt tethered by an unspoken promise: that he belonged with her, and she with him. She locked eyes with him, holding onto the warmth to steady her trembling. She was completely his, her entire being devoted to him.

But over the following weeks, that initial spark wavered. The thrill of shared clipboards and hushed consultations gave way to the steady drone of habit. Charlotte drifted the Health Centre's stark corridors with her phone practically welded to her palm. Every time it vibrated, her pulse vaulted into her throat. The little ellipsis of a pending reply became its own phantom, stoking equal parts hope and fear; when it blinked away without delivering a message, her heart thundered so loudly she half-expected others to hear it down the hall. At exactly 11.30 a.m., she paused, then tapped out: *Where are you?* Fifteen minutes later: *Everything okay?* Each unread text wound her anxiety tighter. One part of her craved honesty; another clung desperately to the numb shelter of ignorance.

Thomas countered her panic with a calm reserve intended to soothe but often felt like salt in a wound. Mornings found him slipping his phone silently into his pocket, offering a courteous nod before he vanished behind the exam room door. Yet by dinnertime—when they settled at their chipped kitchen table, two candles guttering between them—Charlotte could trace the fatigue etched beneath his eyes. One evening, in a quiet plea for closeness, she reached across the table to brush a loose strand of hair from his forehead. Instead of leaning in, he recoiled, pressing his palm to her cheek as though her touch might scorch him.

That fragile tension finally snapped at a family dinner in her childhood home. Her mother arrived bearing a tin of lemon bars—glistening like honeyed gems under the chandelier—

while her father fussed over napkin folds and peppered Thomas with questions about his residency. Thomas answered in a measured low voice that made Charlotte swell with pride—until she caught her mother's gaze, lined with unspoken expectation. She lifted her glass in a timid toast, forcing the same porcelain smile she'd worn since she was small. The tart wine bit at her throat, reminding her of every bitter accommodation she'd swallowed for the sake of peace.

Across the table, Thomas's mother watched serenely, her hands clasped in her lap. She laughed at his anecdotes and offered Charlotte gentle nods. However, each approving glance felt like an invisible noose tightening at Charlotte's neck. Later, in their quiet apartment, Charlotte lay awake, dissecting every smile, every lull in the conversation, as if each were a clue to some hidden rift. Sleep slipped away like a guest sliding out the back door.

In the days that followed, her unease metastasized. She mapped Thomas's daily routine—four hours of sessions, a noon seminar, an evening shift—and waited for his call like a sentry. After nine o'clock, if his voice hadn't

crackled through her speaker, she wandered
the apartment murmuring the time to herself:
ten past. Quarter past. Twenty past.
Then, one rain-soaked evening, the familiar
hum of his car pulled into the lot thirty
minutes late. Charlotte threw open the door,
rain plastering her hair to her face, and collapsed into his arms. Relief broke free in shaky
sobs. He murmured, "I'm sorry", holding her
tight—but Charlotte felt the catch in his breath
and the tremor in his embrace, as though his
own heart longed to break free.

Their fiercest arguments ignited in the fragile
calm before dawn. She would lean over him in
the bed's half--ight, voice shaking as she demanded, "Why didn't you text me back?"
Thomas would sit up slowly, confusion knitting his brows together. "I forgot," he'd say—
quiet, but clipped, as if the conversation itself
was something to escape. But Charlotte heard
only abandonment in those two simple words.
Without thinking, she'd unleash the notebook
of her fears—every line an accusation of un-
worthiness, every flourish a plea for evidence
that he cared. Then he would fold himself
against the pillows beside her, lips offering

150

soft apologies even as his eyes drifted toward the ceiling—as though already retreating to someplace quieter, safer, just out of reach.

One overcast afternoon, Charlotte carried a paper bag into the austere quiet of his studio. She halted by the door's glass panel and watched him lean over a chart, marker in hand, shoulders hunched beneath his white coat. The room smelled of chalk dust and antiseptic, and Charlotte's pulse shivered in her throat. Swallowing, she tapped lightly on the glass before stepping in. She offered him a sandwich wrapped in plain parchment—tuna salad on sourdough—and for a fleeting second, his face softened. But when she reached out to brush a stray crumb from his desk, she caught the rapid tightening of his jaw. After she left, she lay awake imagining him running a frustrated hand through his hair, breathing a silent sigh of relief that she was gone.

Late one night, they curled together on their sagging couch, the television off but the standby light casting a dim blue glow. Charlotte's voice was barely audible: "Tell me you're not going to leave." Thomas shifted beside her, one arm loosening around her shoulders. "Charlotte, I love you," he whispered, his breath warm against her ear. Yet the words felt as fragile as frost on glass—beautiful to see but impossible to grasp.

A few days later, they were having dinner at his parents' house under a bright chandelier that highlighted every tense glance between them. The silverware clattered, and polite conversation flowed, but each pause between Charlotte and Thomas felt like an unspoken accusation.

On the drive back, the rain drummed a rhythmic pattern on the windshield, echoing her growing anxiety. Her hands fidgeted in her lap until the silence became unbearable: "Do you even love me?" she asked, piercing the darkness. Thomas gripped the steering wheel tightly, his knuckles turning white. "Charlotte, please..." he started, but she continued, her words sharp and cutting: "Because I feel like I'm losing you." He let out a long, shaky sigh. "I don't know if I can do this anymore," he admitted so quietly that it seemed like a whisper. She realized she was pushing him, seeking a reaction—a burst of passion that would convince her of his love. She craved the excitement, the intensity, believing that love without passion was destined to fail.

In the days that followed, he retreated behind a wall of distance. His messages became polite and clipped, and his embraces perfunctory. No kiss emoji. No inside jokes. For a second—just a second—Charlotte wondered if he'd already left her in some quiet, irreversible way.

Then came a letter in the mail—an invitation to speak at a medical conference in Sardinia. He explained that he needed space to think, phrasing it with careful gentleness so as not to crush her fragile heart. Charlotte nodded wordlessly, watching him fold shirts into a duffle bag with methodical precision. At the door, she pressed her face against his chest, inhaling his familiar cologne. He stroked her hair and whispered, "I'll be back," before stepping into the drumming rain.

Charlotte leaned against the doorframe, arms crossed over her chest, and watched Thomas pause by the threshold. He lifted a worn duffel bag and slung the fraying canvas strap over one shoulder, the fabric whispering as it slid across his coat. For a moment he froze, half—

turned toward her, and she saw the way his brow furrowed with tension, as if he, too, longed to stay but felt compelled by obligation to leave. Then he reached forward, brushing a loose curl from her forehead with a gentle fingertip. The air between them quivered. His lips brushed her cheek—brief, trembling, as if hesitant to land. Charlotte felt the rough shadow of his stubble graze her skin—gentle, distant, as though he were already halfway down the hallway. Time seemed to stop: the single beat of her heart stretched into eternity. He finally withdrew, stepping back but never entirely pulling away. "Take care of yourself, okay?" His voice was low, deliberate, each word dropped as if testing its weight before release. In that quiet pause that followed, Charlotte found herself craving more—another touch, another second—but only silence answered. She gripped the doorframe tighter, thumb digging into the chipped paint until she sensed the faint give of softened wood beneath her nail. She tried to summon a smile, but it felt brittle in her chest, ready to shatter. "I will," she whispered. Her voice wavered at the edges. "And... you too."

He offered a slow nod, dark eyes reflecting a storm she couldn't read. Then he hoisted the duffel once more, shifted his stance, and slipped past her into the corridor.

Charlotte remained in the doorway for long moments after he was gone, her spine pressed against cool wood. The hallway light flickered on overhead, inert and unforgiving, illuminating her solitude as though she were an exhibit in a glass case. Every sound—the scratch of her shoe against the threshold, the creak of the floorboard—resounded in her ears. Her heart thrummed so loudly she could almost will it to stop.

She knew she ought to move, to step inside and close the door against the emptiness. But her legs felt rooted, as if encased in damp cement. Only when the relentless ticking of the kitchen clock crept into her consciousness— each sharp click anchoring her to the moment—did she manage to pull herself away. Inside, she trailed one sleeve along the countertop, leaving a slender smear of fabric on the polished surface. As if, in that small gesture, she might leave behind some fragment of herself, safe until he returned.

Silence moved into the apartment like an unbidden guest, spreading its chill across their once-shared bed. The pillow beside her still bore the faint imprint of his head. In that hush she finally saw the cage she had built around them—bars constructed of doubt, fear, and her relentless need for reassurance. As thunder rumbled in the distance, Charlotte closed her eyes and made a vow: if their love was ever to stand on solid ground again, she would first learn to stand firmly on her own.

~

That first evening, she plunged into her duties at Hayfield Health Centre, seeking solace in the flurry of activity. Her office was a small oasis, a pastel sanctuary drenched in soft blushes and soothing mint greens. The walls were adorned with an array of framed certificates and motivational quotes in elegant, looping script, each perfectly with white frames gleaming and utterly devoid of fingerprints. A vase of fresh peonies graced the corner of her desk, their petals a tender blush hue, as if they were gentle cheeks, shyly blushing under the clinical fluorescent light. Her desk was a study in minimalism and order, holding only the essentials—a sleek glass pen holder, a stack of pastel notepads ready for thoughts still to be penned, and a ceramic cup decorated with tiny daisies, still radiating warmth from her morning tea. It was a space that exuded an air of innocent tranquillity, where chaos was banished, and control reigned supreme—a soft cocoon with a precision so exacting it felt almost childlike in its simplicity. She methodically rearranged stacks of patient charts on her desk until they formed perfect rows; she delved into case files long past dinner, her eyes tracing every line with meticulous care; she scrubbed the break room sink with a toothbrush, her knuckles blanching from the effort as she tirelessly coaxed away stubborn stains.

But at midnight, when the last custodian left and the corridors fell hush, the silence slithered back in through the corridor vents and curled around her ankles like smoke. She retreated to her apartment, sank onto her sagging sofa, and wrapped a threadbare blanket unevenly around her knees. The only illumination came from her phone as she waited for a message. Her breath hitched each time the device buzzed, only to sigh in disappointment when it proved to be a notification from work or a harmless social update. Then, just as she began to drift toward restless sleep, her phone buzzed again—a single vibration that jolted her upright. Fingers trembling, she unlocked the screen.

"Made it to the conference. Busy day. Hope all is well." No exclamation mark. No affectionate nickname. Just few precise words, as impersonal as a typed receipt. Charlotte felt a knot twisting beneath her ribs. Her thumb hovered over the keyboard, unsure of how to express all she wanted to say. After a pause, she typed, "Glad you're safe. Miss you." It wasn't entirely true, or at least not the main reason she sent it. She hoped to provoke an "I miss you too" in return, seeking validation for the connection she lacked. What she really missed was the sensation of being needed, of being a means to an end. The sound of the message sending echoed through the quiet room like a hollow drum.

Night after night she lay awake, pillow damp with tears she refused to wipe away. The bathroom faucet leaked in a steady drip—drip, drip—each plink echoing through her skull, reminding her of the widening gap growing between them. With every buzz of her phone, her stomach clenched. Three words here, four words there, never enough to bridge the miles that yawed between Charlotte's hopes and Thomas's absence. She pictured him in a vast lecture hall, the lights dimmed so the slides gleamed on the screen. Rows of stiff chairs surrounded him, and he leaned forward, pen poised over crisp pages, jotting notes for an audience of strangers. But who, she wondered, was he writing for if not her?

~

The phone rang, breaking the stillness of her apartment. She hesitated, then answered. His voice crackled with distance and unsettling closeness.

"Hey. I'm staying two more nights. There's a follow-up session," he announced decisively. After a pause, he added, "Hope that's okay." She moved the phone away, letting the receiver drop back, its sound echoing through the room. Her fingers clenched the sofa fabric, the air feeling oppressive, her heartbeat a dull thud. *Hope that's okay...* As if she had any say in that.

He had spoken nonchalantly, as if she were just a visitor in his life, not its centre. She closed her eyes against the sly burn of tears. She wanted to scold him, to demand explanations, to recall each lonely hour she'd spent waiting. But all that rose to her lips was a silent plea carried on a sigh.

~

When Thomas finally returned, Charlotte was in her robe, her hair half-brushed, staring

160

blankly at the wall above the sofa. She heard his footsteps before the door opened: a soft scrape of wheels on tile, the faint scrape of suitcase casings. The door swung wide before she could rise.

There he stood, framed in the doorway by the cool, fluorescent light of the building's lobby. His shirt was rumpled in that familiar way that said he'd travelled hard but still wanted to look at least half-decent for her. A fresh wave of cologne—pine and citrus—drifted toward her, crisp and grounded like a forest breeze after rain. His cheeks were sun-kissed, his hair tousled by airport drafts, his eyes lighter somehow, as if the weight he'd carried had been lifted. Charlotte's throat tightened. Her breath caught, and for the first time in weeks, she felt her heart's knot loosen. The distance dissolved in an instant. "Hey," he whispered, shyly, as he set down his bags and stepped fully into the apartment's dim warmth.

She rose on trembling feet, reached up onto her tiptoes, and he lowered his head to meet her halfway. His arms were warm and solid around her, an anchor that banished every lingering shadow of loneliness. He pressed his forehead to hers; his breath tickled her cheek like the gentle brush of a bird's wing.

"I'm sorry I was distant," he murmured, fingers tracing slow, reassuring circles at the small of her back. "I needed space to think. But I'm here now."

Charlotte tilted her face into his palm, eyes closing as relief and love stirred in her chest like slow-burning embers. She could smell the faint trace of pine on his collar and knew she wouldn't let it go. She didn't ask about Italy, about why he'd stayed longer or texted so rarely. None of it mattered anymore. All that mattered was this moment.

He kissed her forehead, lingering as though imprinting her warmth into his memory, then hovered for a heartbeat over her lips before he closed the gap. The kiss was gentle but insistent, full of the longing of all the empty days and nights they'd spent apart. When they finally broke apart, Charlotte ran her fingers along his jaw, committing the curve of his profile, the heat of his skin, to memory.

Outside the window, dusk had deepened into a soft indigo, and a single star glimmered, pale and hopeful. Charlotte drew in a steady breath and let it out slowly, feeling it anchoring her to the present. The apartment felt cozier now, wrapped in the promise of this reunion. She had lit candles that night. Lavender and rose. The same scent he once said reminded him of home. She hoped he'd notice. The frayed edges of their separation would unravel in time, she knew that. But for tonight, this embrace was enough. In his arms, she believed—truly believed—that everything would be all right.

3.
SALT

"The world breaks everyone, and afterward many are strong at the broken places." — Ernest Hemingway

A solitary figure rounded the bend onto the quayside, and the world seemed to seize in that moment between land and sea. Salt-laden gusts crashed into him like icy ribbons, each inhalation an electric shock that pricked his nostrils and left a glitter of spray clinging to his eyelashes. Underfoot, centuries-worn planks moaned in protest, betraying the weight of each step as tidal waters, whipped to foam, struck the quay with a relentless swoosh. Clumps of drifting algae and coils of seaweed swirled at his boots, carried by the rhythm of the tide as if beckoning him onward. Overhead, the iron grey sky teemed with gulls—white-winged ghosts wheeling and shrieking, their cries slicing through the damp hush of morning. Scattered about lay hanks of rope, emptied wooden crates askew, and the sour odour of rotting timber mingled with acrid diesel fumes rising from trawlers at rest. Beyond this clutter, the true magnet of the port awaited: a colossal vessel of steel and shadow moored just beyond the smaller fishing skiffs. Its hull rose like a steel cliff face, pockmarked with rivets, and stained with rust that bled orange streaks where saltwater had slowly devoured the paint. Onto its broad deck fifty tiers of multi-coloured containers were stacked in dizzying barricades—burnt sienna next to cobalt blue, sun-bleached canary yellow, forest green mottled with black. They loomed overhead like a city forged from iron, its streets and alleys hidden behind smooth, featureless walls. Even at idle, the great ship exhaled a soft, pulsating thrum, a low vibration that seeped through the planks and seemed to awaken the dock itself.

He drew in a ragged breath, his heart pounding at the vast indifference of the machine before him. The harbour of his island home— sun-scorched bays he'd known all his life—had always felt intimate, shaped by familiar tides and human hands. This place, by contrast, was an arena of giants, its scale a reminder that he was no more than a grain of sand on the shore. And yet, in that resonant hum, he heard an echo of something ancient stirring in his chest. He had come this far to answer that summons, to leave behind the sheltered coves of Mezzaluna Bay and step into the boundless unknown.

Light from a chipped metal canopy flickered overhead as he entered a small hall. The harsh glare revealed rows of weathered counters behind which immigration officers dozed beneath stacks of forms. A single man sat upright; his face drained of interest. "Your papers," he snapped, eyes never rising. Wordlessly, the newcomer placed his documents on the scratched laminate surface. The officer flipped through them with clinical detachment, then leaned forward, voice flat and precise: "Name?" There was a pause. Feeling the officer's gaze like a blade, he spoke, clear but measured, "Carlo De Paoli."
A moment later, the rubber stamp met the embossed seal with a crack that echoed through the silent room. No words of welcome

followed—only a curt nod and an outstretched hand indicating the gangway beyond. He squared his shoulders and set off across the quay, stepping deeper into the ship's yawning shadow. At the water's edge, a narrow plank bridged the gap between dock and deck, paint peeling away in long curls. It bobbed with every swell, and as he stepped onto the grainy wood, he had to steady himself by the coarse rope railing, knuckles turning white. The plank groaned beneath his weight; brine spattered his trousers with cold urgency.

Even now, as he pressed forward, memories rose unbidden from home: a cluster of cottages folded against emerald hills; the sharp tang of salt on his father's jacket and the soft thud of clay lamp striking stone. At twilight, the village gathered on the pebbled shore, women in scarlet and saffron swirling like living flames around crackling bonfires while guitars thrummed and voices wove songs older than memory. Under starlit rafters of wind and pine, full—bodied tuna glimmered in returning boats—silver leviathans coveted by mainland traders who carried tales of chiming clocks, distant bazaars, and drums that never ceased their pulse, the last remnants of the century gone. He had hung on each word, each new vision fanning a flame of longing to breach the horizon he had always seen as a boundary for someone else.

The plank gave one last shudder beneath him as he hauled himself onto the cool steel deck. A tall figure in a navy blue uniform waited, shoulders squared and face set in a half-smile that held nothing but impatience.
"Welcome aboard," the man said with a crisp voice, then turned on his heel and disappeared into a yawning hatchway without giving Carlo a chance to reply. His suitcase rattled on the deck plates as he hurried after the retreating form. Inside, the vessel revealed itself as a maze of narrow corridors lit by dim, yellow bulbs that flickered with every step. The air was cool, spiced with the scent of gearbox oil, hydraulic fluid, and damp steel. His soles clanked against grated metal walkways as he followed the uniformed man's footsteps deeper into the ship's iron entrails. Beneath their feet, the engines' subtle thrum had grown into a steady, living heartbeat.

At last they reached a small cabin carved into that steel fortress. The door protested on its hinges, revealing an uninviting space. Cream-painted walls attempted a gesture at calm, but the narrow bunk, topped by a thin, lumpy mattress, looked more prison than refuge. Opposite, a chipped wooden desk bore a lamp whose missing bulb left the wiring exposed. Through the porthole, a massive orange container filled the view, slicing the cabin in rusty bands of light and shadow.

"Drop your things and change into that," the uniformed man directed, gesturing at a neatly folded outfit on the desk: grey canvas trousers and a pale blue shirt stiff with starch and the tang of machine oil. "Report to the bridge for introductions." He slipped away so silently that Carlo half-wondered if he'd melted into the steel walls.

Carlo's upper body, laid bare to the cabin's cool, dense atmosphere, was a tribute to the years he had spent labouring under sudrenched coastlines. The contours of his body were sharply defined, sculpted by countless hours of labour. His skin, a warm bronze hue, was weathered beyond his youthful years, carrying the tactile impressions of salt and wind. It was a map of his life's journey, with stories written in the subtle lines at his shoulders and the firm, muscular planes of his chest. Sparse but robust dark hair adorned his expansive chest, forming a tapering line over his sternum and down his abdomen, where the firm ridges of muscle suggested a life spent hauling in heavy nets and deftly scaling the rigging of ships. His physique was ruggedly hewn, embodying a raw, distinct, and unapologetically masculine vigour that spoke of strength and resilience. Each movement steadied him. He straightened his collar, locked his jaw, and stepped back into the corridor. The narrow passageway seemed to pulse around him, pipes tracing ghostly veins overhead, steel walls pressing close. The engines' drone vibrated beneath his feet, warming the plates enough to make the air thick.

When he pushed open the bridge door, a hush fell over him. The vast chamber was bathed in natural light pouring through floor-to-ceiling windows, revealing the port in motion beyond: cranes stretching like herons over concrete piers, cargo trucks weaving between stacked containers, smaller freighters slipping past in silent procession. Inside, the room felt detached from the world's cacophony, as though he'd stepped through a membrane into perfect stillness. At the centre stood a man whose broad back was turned to the doorway. His uniform was impeccable; polished brass insignia gleamed on his shoulders. His hands—thick, knotted, and calloused—rested on the control console, fingers flexing in time with the bridge's soft hum. A crew member at the side cleared his throat. "Captain, the new cadet has arrived."

Silence hovered like a blade as the Captain turned. Dark eyes—cold as river stones—settled on Carlo with a scrutiny that made his spine stiffen. Moments passed before a low, gravelly voice broke the quiet. "You must be De Paoli," the Captain said, his gaze flicking over the young seaman's creased uniform and uncertain posture. "From one of those fishing villages, I hear. You understand this isn't your father's small boat. We're a cargo operation—precision, discipline, no room for error."

Carlo swallowed hard. "Yes, Captain."

The Captain's lips curved in something like

approval before he turned back to his instruments, adjusting a dial with a single, precise motion. "Then get to work," he said. "Follow orders, stay sharp, and you might just make it through our run." There was no room for delay or small talk. Carlo realized he had entered a realm completely removed from the humanity bustling outside the large windows of the ship's Bridge. He was gradually sinking into a wild, untamed expanse where creatures roamed freely, beyond the reach of societal norms.

Dismissed, Carlo nodded once and left the bridge with a young deckhand who wordlessly led him back into the labyrinth.

Over the following days he was assigned to the lower holds, where corridors of containers stood like steel crypts. The air was stifling— thick with heat, oil vapor, and sweat. Electric lights twinkled overhead, casting jittery shadows that danced across bulging cargo seals. His duties: inspect each seal, tighten every latch, secure taut lines against shifting loads. He learned to crank the heavy ratchet wrench until his fingertips burned, to haul steel cables that bit into his palms, to recognize the

ominous hiss of escaping hydraulic pressure before any accident could strike. Around him, the crew moved in muted concert—men of varied tongues and tanned, weather-etched skins. Tattoos of anchors, compasses, and sea serpents curled along their forearms. Conversation came sparingly, broken by guttural phrases and the occasional barked order.
At night, when the bridge lights dimmed and the hull settled into its deeper rhythms, the engines' relentless pulse was his only lullaby. The narrow bunk waited cold beneath a porthole blocked by another container; stars forever hidden.

In those long, twilight-blended hours, memories of home pressed in on him: the warmth of bonfire embers on the beach, the heady scent of myrtle blooming on hillside trails, the lilting verses of ballad singers echoing over gentle waves. There, the sky was an endless dome spangled with stars—here, the heavens had been walled off by steel decks.
He remembered the narrow cobblestone alleys snaking between pastel-coloured walls, the stones worn smooth by generations of hard soles. Faint traces of salt and sun clung to the

cracked limewash, soft green lichen edging every crevice. Above him, laundry lines wove a colourful canopy, sheets snapping in the breeze like the sails of fishing boats rocking in the harbour. He could still hear the groan of rusted iron gates, the metallic clatter of copper pans in open kitchens, and the low murmur of old women leaning from second-story windows, shawls drawn tight, exchanging the day's gossip. From the terraced slopes above the village, the view opened onto a patchwork of grapevines and terracotta rooftops. The air would be heavy with wild rosemary and the sweet, resinous scent of juniper. Gnarled olive trees gripped the rocky earth, their twisted branches whispering secrets to the mistral as it swept in from the north, setting their silver leaves to restless fluttering. Beyond the orchards, the sea stretched barefoot to the horizon, its surface shifting through every shade of blue and green.

In his mind's ear he heard the deep toll of bronze bells from the town's church, with its yellow walls, standing tall on the main piazza, and their solemn peals rolling down to the quay where fishermen mended nets in the dying light. The sea there was a barrier but a cradle—warm and breathing with the tides, its clarity revealing white pebbles and darting silver fish beneath the surface. Gulls cried sharp above the boats, their wings glittering like fragments of sunlight against the vast blue. He had known those waters intimately, diving from the jagged rocks that framed the cove, his body slicing through the cool depths like the sleek sea bream he and his father chased. He felt again the sting of salt on his skin as he hauled the day's catch onto the stones, the sun scorching his shoulders as he dragged dripping nets ashore. And when the sea turned liquid gold at dusk, he and the others would gather around the fire, their rough harmonies rising in unison as guitars thrummed and dancing flames cast wild shadows on the cliff face.

Yet as he worked, something within hardened like the hull around him. He had chosen this path, to leave the embrace of Mezzaluna Bay for the promise of horizons unseen. If the labour was brutal, it was honest—and the deep-toned heartbeat reminded him that he was part of something immense, something greater than any story he had heard on the shore. His hands grew calloused and unflinching; his back steeled itself against strain. He devoured the cargo manifest, navigated by memory the ship's twisting passages, answered commands with crisp precision.

One morning, as Carlo emerged from the hold, breathless from tightening the last bolt, he met Captain Vincenzo Garofalo's gaze in the hallway. The Captain's eyes, steady and piercing like steel, seemed to scrutinize Carlo intensely. His hazel eyes, framed by age lines, sparkled in the dim light, their focus sharp and unwavering. Garofalo's stubble, dark and coarse, covered his round cheeks and double chin, suggesting he hadn't shaved in days. His thinning, curly hair was turning grey and rested untamed on his forehead, clearly overdue for a trim.

Garofalo's face was marked by the sun, with a deep, rugged tan interrupted by pale crow's feet at the corners of his eyes. His uniform collar, too tight to be fully buttoned, gaped just below his throat, revealing sparse, wiry chest hairs protruding defiantly. The stiff fabric pressed against his thick neck, hinting at a

man who had outgrown his fit long ago.
The Captain's eyes lingered on Carlo's sweat-streaked uniform before rising to assess the young sailor, who stood a bit more proudly. Without a word exchanged, Carlo felt a shift— a reluctant sign of acceptance from the man who personified the ship's spirit.

~

The endless days aboard the MV Lawrence unfurled like a sea-stained tapestry. Each sunrise bled into the next in a relentless cycle of grey light and grinding steel, as if the world beyond the portholes had ceased to exist. From the moment Carlo set foot on her cold decks, an uncanny unreality enveloped him: corridors stretched on forever, engine rooms echoed with unseen giants, and time itself seemed to pool in dark corners, lost to memory. Deep beneath the waterline, the ship's engines pounded with a metallic heartbeat that resonated through floor plates and bones alike. In that ceaseless vibration Carlo drifted between waking dreams and half-formed dread, each dawn arriving as a challenge he scarcely felt prepared to meet.

The morning light came through the dirty windows in pale streaks, lighting up the lower deck doors as they opened loudly. This noise signalled the start of another workday: hard work for every day of the week for as long as the Lawrence sailed the crisp seas. Sweat mixed with fresh grease, creating a smell that stuck to everyone's clothes and filled every breath in that cramped space of creaking metal.

For Carlo, the ship's constant noise was both annoying and soothing. Before the morning light touched the sky, Carlo forced himself out of his small bed. His joints ached from the cold, and his mind was foggy with tiredness and the engine's hum. He shuffled along the deck toward the breakfast room. Inside, a row of bright light bulbs hung from the ceiling, shining on a long table covered in what used to be a clean white tablecloth, now covered in grease spots, dark spills, and crusty patches that wouldn't come off, no matter how hard you scrubbed.

At one end, the officers gathered like gilded priests around steaming croissants, sugar-dusted buns, and thin slices of ham wrapped around orderly wedges of butter. Further along, the quality thinned: stale biscuits perched precariously on chipped plates, fruit peering out of copper bowls tarnished by neglect. Carlo made his way to the bench at the far end—the seat assigned to him—where a single rock-hard roll sat next to a thermos of lukewarm tea. Each crumbles chew, each tepid gulp, was a mute confession of his place in the shipboard hierarchy: insignificance dressed as sustenance.

After days of clenched teeth and growling stomach, Carlo discovered a narrow window of opportunity. He learned the rhythm of the ship and timed his approach to the saloon just before the officers and stewards converged in a hungry throng. On those rare mornings, the cook was the only one around: a squat man dusted in flour, whose weathered hands coaxed dough into existence as if performing a hallowed rite. When the baker's attention drifted, Carlo's fingers closed around a sugar-crusted pastry—still warm and steaming—and he slipped back onto the corridor.

Outside, the wind carried the tang of salt spray; below, the disturbed foam churned in the ship's wake like restless spirits outraged at being disturbed. Perched on a coil of rope high above the waves, Carlo tore into the pastry, letting sweetness flood his senses in a precious heartbeat, while the broad horizon gleamed with sudden, fragile hope.

Reality, however, returned with unforgiving insistence. From that stolen moment until dusk, Carlo's hours were claimed by unrelenting labour: he scraped away forty years of peeling paint from deck railings, each stroke uncovering layers of rust until his shoulders burned and his scraper risked slipping from numb fingers. He climbed narrow ladders to the tank decks, measuring oil and ballast on slick steel coated in condensation. In the stifling cargo holds he coiled rope thicker than his arm, sweat pounding at his temples until his skin crackled with grit. In lockers black as tombs, he dusted off crates of long-forgotten freight. There was no chore too filthy for officers' scrutiny: a loose bolt here, a misplaced rag there, every bead of sweat, every blistered callus, was proof positive that Carlo was nothing but an expendable cog in a vessel that ground men down until they snapped.

When at last the Lawrence edged into port, Carlo found himself on the bow before sunrise, braced against a salt—lashed wind that cut through layers of wool like a razor. He looped thick mooring lines around bollards, knuckles white despite stout gloves; he cranked winches under a sun already climbing, turning the steel decks into mirrors of blistering glare. No festive welcome attended his crossing onto the quay, only the cold nods of dockworkers who saw the Lawrence as nothing more than another floating machine. Even amid such drudgery, Carlo's stoic endurance began to earn grudging respect, now fellow crew members offered stiff nods as they crossed his path. Rumours of his reliability spread from engine rooms to mess decks until even the brashest deckhands tipped their caps in his direction. And then, as if summoned by the murmur of his growing reputation, Captain Garofalo entered Carlo's life.

Garofalo was a living mountain, as wide as a furnace door and nearly as menacing. His voice shook the corridors, crashing against steel bulkheads like thunder, sending even hardened seafarers scuttling away in fear. Whispers of his cruelty followed him—tales of men driven to despair, officers shamed before their peers, careers obliterated by his icy scorn. At home, rumour had it, he surrendered every ounce of authority to his meticulous wife; aboard the Lawrence, he reclaimed it with predatory relish, treating each crew member like a tool to be honed—or discarded. One evening, just as the western sky ignited in brilliant oranges and copper hues, Carlo permitted himself a rare moment of calm. He leaned against the sun-bleached rail, eyes closed, feeling the dying light play across his face, and listened to the distant cries of seabirds gliding on the sea breeze. Then a shadow fell—a long, dark silhouette stretching across his shoulders. He opened a single eye to find Garofalo looming over him, silent until the last smudge of daylight vanished beyond the horizon. "De Paoli," the Captain said, voice low and deliberate. Carlo's heart pounded as if

183

protesting his audacity. Garofalo's gaze drifted to the waterline's faint shimmer, as if weighing Carlo's worth against the indifferent sea. He spoke, tossing a gauntlet at Carlo's feet in the form of few simple words: "Don't make mistakes." Then, with a final, inscrutable stare, he turned away, vanishing into the gathering gloom and leaving Carlo alone with uncertainty: had he been threatened—or acknowledged?

After that, every movement Carlo made felt scrutinized. Garofalo's laughter—sharp and derisive—rippled through bulkheads whenever a crew member faltered. Each mishap drew mocking whispers that trailed behind Carlo like smoke. Even the battered meteorology book he studied while on watch on the bridge became target for cynical jibes. "You think you'll study your way off this deathtrap, boy?" Garofalo sneered one morning. "Out here it's muscle or misery—and I don't see you coming out on top." His words dripped with contempt, as though the Captain resented Carlo's very existence. What had happened?

When night fell, Carlo slipped away with the deckhands: lanky Indonesians swapping jokes in rapid-fire Bahasa, stocky Filipinos humming folk tunes as they polished winches, sturdy Samoan bosun mates offering smokes from crumpled packs. In the ship's cramped, shadowed corners—behind coils of rope in the aft hold, beneath tarpaulins in the forecastle, huddled beside rumbling bulkheads—they formed a loose ring of camaraderie. A shared cigarette's glow or the pluck of a battered guitar was their only taste of freedom aboard this steel leviathan. Here, rank melted into laughter, authority's sharp edges blurred by tobacco smoke and the steady beat of sea shanties. They sat cross-legged on grease-stained deck plates, faces lit by a flickering storm lantern, voices rising and falling in a dozen tongues— each accent a heartbeat from lands beyond the hull. Poker games unfolded on overturned crates: cards slapped down with theatrical flair, coins and crumpled bills passed around as tales of distant beaches and late night bar fights wove through the air. Someone always had a harmonica or a weathered ukulele, its strings plucked by the same calloused fingers that hauled lines and tightened bolts by day. Their melodies—sometimes mournful, sometimes mischievous—drifted into the ship's dark recesses, a ghostly chorus echoing off steel walls and rust-streaked girders. Meanwhile, the officers—the straight-backed, pale-skinned Europeans—retreated into private, airless cabins bathed in cold fluorescent light. Off duty, they clung to their ranks as if shedding the stiff collar of authority would strip them of command. They dined alone or in hushed tones, faces set in hard, unreadable lines, the ship's hierarchy clinging to them like a second skin. Their quarters echoed with the hollow clink of silverware on porcelain, the soft rustle of turning pages, and the occasional crackle of a radio tuned to distant voices. They paced in circles, mentally reciting protocol and rank, each precise movement a reminder of their fragile hold on power. They seemed to fear the humanity they rigidly enforced—terrified that one unguarded laugh or shared drink might shatter the brittle glass of their authority. They wrapped themselves in titles, stripes, and insignia, clutching the illusion of control like a lifeline. In their isolation, Carlo recognized the same unease that had gripped generations of men who wielded power not from strength but from the unspoken terror that, without their uniforms, they'd be no more significant than the creaking steel and rusting bolts around them. This self-imposed solitude mirrored the fragility of their status ashore—a world where straight white men, long accustomed to unchallenged dominance, now shrank back into offices and boardrooms as their power slipped away like sand through a clenched fist. They mistook distance for strength and silence for respect, blind to the vibrant, unrestrained humanity thriving just beyond their cabin doors.

And so the hierarchy endured—a brittle cage of their own making—while the deckhands laughed, sang, and spun stories of moonlit beaches and open skies, their voices rising into the darkened air, the only living thing stirring in the ship's iron heart.

Then, like a mirage, shore leave materialized on the horizon once more. The MV *Lawrence* lay at anchor in rada, gently swaying on the swells off Singapore's coast, its rusty hull groaning with the rhythm of the tide. Beyond the churning water, the skyline thrust upward like a jagged crown of glass and steel, spires of silver and mirrored façades capturing the sun's final, fiery rays. In the distance, Marina Bay Sands stood colossal and inverted atop its three pillars, while the Singapore Flyer traced slow, deliberate circles against an orange-pink sky. The scene was almost too pristine—every line crisp, every reflection perfect, as if lifted from a postcard. Carlo's pulse raced as the engines rumbled beneath him, a low vibration that promised freedom. He pictured the port's chaos: forklifts hissing like angry serpents, cranes clanging as they hoisted steel containers skyward, engines roaring through the thick tropical heat. Even here, he could glimpse neon signs flickering in the humid dusk, their colours fractured across the restless harbour. He imagined the streets beyond: hawker stalls steaming with sizzling meats and spiced noodles, beer bottles clinking on chipped Formica, the acrid bite of chili smoke clinging to sweat-slick skin. He longed for the electric pulse of crowded alleyways thick with the scent of fried fish and garlic, voices overlapping in a thousand languages. Twenty days at sea had left him starved for that human tumult.

As he made for the gangway, his boots clanking on salt-eaten grates, he stole a final look at the horizon. The tender sat alongside, battered, and dented, already jammed with men joking and slapping backs, their faces bright with anticipation of cold beer and soft beds. Then he saw the cabin's interior: every seat claimed by his crewmates; shoulders pressed together in the stifling heat. And there, impossibly broad-shouldered, and impassive, sat Captain Garofalo, arms crossed like iron bars. "De Paoli," the Captain boomed, his voice hammering through the engine's hum, "sorry—the boat's full. You stay aboard." The words struck Carlo like a physical blow, each syllable driving rusted nails into his chest. He opened his mouth to argue, but the tender's engine roared to life, prompted by Garofalo's firm tap on the cabin roof, its hull cutting through the water with a hiss that drowned out his plea. He gripped the cold, pitted railing as the boat pulled away, his shipmates' smirking faces, whispering and speculating, slipping into shadow.

Each bob of the tender's bow twisted the knife

deeper. The city lights blurred before him, a neon constellation receding with every churning wave. He felt tears press behind his eyes but forced them back, jaw clenched, as the last glow of the skyline vanished. The cranes continued their mechanical groans, indifferent predators swinging steel arms in the night, while the MV Lawrence hummed its unending lament.

Frosty and unfeeling, the ocean suddenly felt like a cage—an expanse that had claimed his youth, his dreams, and now his last taste of human warmth.

On the Lawrence, narrow passageways and the ever-present rumble of the engine room greeted him like an old jailer. Gauges hissed, valves growled, pistons thudded in a claustrophobic symphony of confinement. Even small kindnesses—a handed cigarette, a brief nod—were shadowed by caution. *Best keep your distance. The Captain's eyes are everywhere.* Still, Carlo pressed on, transforming grief into fuel and exhaustion into determination.

Anticipating Garofalo's disdain before the order was even spoken, Carlo volunteered to clean vent lines in hold C—an assignment so foul that every other man had balked. He descended into the bowels of the ship, working methodically until the ducts gleamed. Emerge he did, filthy but triumphant, expecting praise. Instead, he found Garofalo's brow lift in surprised approval. For the briefest moment, the Captain's smirk softened, and Carlo felt a fierce spark of victory flare within him—small, incandescent, almost sacred against the surrounding gloom. That fragile spark, however, was snuffed out in a single, violent breath. Late one night, a hard rap on his cabin door jolted Carlo from sleep. He opened it to find Garofalo filling the frame, backlit by the dim corridor lamp. "De Paoli," the Captain said, voice dropping like an anchor, "we need to talk." Inside the cramped office—no larger than a steel sarcophagus—Garofalo prowled like a predator, eyes flicking over Carlo's scant possessions: the thin wool blanket rolled at the foot of the bunk, the sepia photograph of his family pinned above it, the battered leather notebook packed with weather charts and half-finished poems. Finally, Garofalo halted, face inches from Carlo's, and spoke with unnerving calm: "You've been working hard. But

I think you can do better."

Carlo's throat tightened. "I'm doing my best, Captain."

At that the Captain's thin lips curved in a cold, cruel smile. In a single, lightning—fast motion he clamped his massive hand around Carlo's shoulder. Pain blossomed in Carlo's arm, a white-hot flare lancing to his spine. "You think you're better than the rest," Garofalo hissed, voice low as a grinding winch. "Because you come from an island, you think you'll glide through this life." The grip tightened until Carlo's teeth ground together. The world contracted to steel walls and Captain's searing breath. Then, mercifully, the pressure released. Garofalo straightened with a grunt of satisfaction. "That's more like it," he muttered. "Remember your place, De Paoli. I run this ship. I can break you as easily as I've broken the others." With that final verdict he turned heel, letting the door slam shut like a guillotine.

Back in his cabin, Carlo sank to his bunk, back pressed against cold steel, each pulse pounding in his ears. Garofalo's promise, *I can break you*, reverberated through the metal walls like a death knell. Yet beneath the burn in his shoulder and the weight settling in his chest, something flickered: a stubborn ember of defiance. He would not merely endure. He would learn to resist. In that cramped, petrol-scented room, amid threat and isolation, Carlo tasted the first true hope he had known aboard the MV Lawrence.

~

Garofalo's arrival didn't so much as announce itself as it detonated the ship's very core. From the moment the hatch swung wide on his broad shoulders, a tremor coursed through every rivet and joist, through every marrow in each sailor's bones. His shoes struck the metal with a slow, inexorable thump, his uniform—cap gleaming like obsidian, jacket starched into a deathly sheen, trousers so sharply creased they might slice the air—spoke of rigid order and ruthless precision. On the bridge, Garofalo reigned supreme in this vacuum of sound—none dared to breach the oppressive stillness he imposed. So, when he finally spoke, his voice cut through the silence like an eviscerating blade. To stand in his presence was to feel solidarity evaporate, suspicion cleave through camaraderie, and trust shatter into fragments more painful than steel. Beneath an unrelenting sun that beat upon the deck for weeks, tension had simmered in hidden recesses like embers beneath ash— Garofalo crouched on the brink of cruelty, patient, methodical, utterly merciless.

Carlo De Paoli lay prostrate over the chart room's steel_topped table, his brow almost grazing the yellowed parchment of the navigation charts, their edges smeared with fingerprints and wear. He held his pencil with knuckles white, scanning each waypoint with obsessive care. Radar blips danced on a dim screen to his left; GPS coordinates flickered in neon green; gyrocompass arcs cut perfect circles across the chart. He closed his eyes and tuned into the subtle vibrato of turbines far below. Temperature, humidity, barometric pressure. A rasp of uniform fabric on steel made his heart spike. "Confident in these coordinates, De Paoli?" Garofalo's voice slithered through the doorway—soft, deliberate, poisonous. Carlo froze, pencil trembling in midair, his pulse hammering in his ears like surf on rocks. He straightened, spine rigid with forced composure. "Yes, sir," he managed, voice hoarse, throat thick with dread. "Cross-checked them twice, sir."

Garofalo stepped forward, each movement measured. The Captain's lip curled into a sneer as he snatched the chart from the table. Carlo watched numbly as the paper quivered under those iron fingers, then slapped back onto the steel surface—graphite streaking like a wound. "We'll see how long your precious precision lasts," Garofalo muttered, eyes glittering with the anticipation of collapse. Every inflection was a gauntlet thrown, every glance an accusation sharpened to pierce the soul. Carlo's fingers clenched around his pencil until his nails bit into his palms. He knew the coordinates were flawless—could recite them blindfolded—but Garofalo's hunger for dominance was insatiable. Which flaw would he unearth today? What pretext would he wield to crush Carlo's quiet diligence? But, most of all, why?

Anxiety buzzed within him like a hive of frantic flies. He swallowed hard, abandoned the bridge in hurried retreat, and descended toward the bow's labyrinthine passages until he found the paint locker.

Inside the cramped tin cell, the acrid tang of turpentine and enamel struck his lungs like acid. Shelves bowed under half-spent cans of primer, lacquer, rust inhibitor; jars of brushes bristled like captive spines; pigment-smeared rags drooped from hooks. Carlo pressed his back against the cold bulkhead, sliding down until his knees met the rough floor. His hands trembled on his thighs, and behind closed lids he let tears blaze trails down his cheeks—hot, insistent rivulets that hissed softly as they hit the grimy steel. In that haze of solvents and paint fumes, his fragile composure shattered. But somewhere amid the breakdown, a single ember of defiance flared—small, stubborn, and fiercely alive.

In the days that followed, Carlo's voice grew scarce, reserved only for essential commands. He found refuge in the ritual of paint: meticulously sanding away rust, blending pigments until they captured the exact depth of naval blue or the muted redness of oxidized steel. Hours slipped by in wordless focus, the whisper of brush against metal a meditation that kept memories of the bridge at bay. The paint locker turned into his refuge, the aroma of enamel and thinner acted as a barrier against his fears. It was a quiet, secluded, and overlooked spot where he could retreat and catch glimpses of who he used to be.

~

Then came that afternoon on the starboard wing when the fragile truce collapsed. Perched midway to the antenna deck, Carlo leaned over a small leather notebook, translating the latest course corrections into tidy bullet points. Overhead, the sun blazed with cruel intensity, transforming the ocean into a seething mirror of cerulean fire. A lone flying fish arced in metallic splendour before slipping back into the endless blue. Above him, the lattice of steel masts and cables loomed like the skeleton of some great beast. At its top, Garofalo held court, sprawled in a battered deck chair that bore sweat-stains and salt crusts. He lounged at ease in dark trousers and a black polo—at least at first—but then, as though peeling away dignity as easily as clothing, he shed layer after layer until only a pair of burgundy speedos clung to his thick thighs. His physique was that of an overgrown toddler, his round belly pushing outward like a taut drum, sprinkled with sparse, wiry chest hair that revolted around prominent, rosy nipples, which jutted out as if caught in a perpetual state of tension. A darker trail of hair descended from his outward belly button, carving a path down to the tightly stretched fabric of his speedos, where his manhood bulged for space, pressing awkwardly against the thin material. The bulge left little to the imagination—a dense, lumpy mass with prominent testicles and a hint of his shaft tucked to the left, creating an unintentional but undeniable display of masculinity. His armpits, dark and damp, revealed coarse tufts of hair that peeked rebelliously from the sides as he raised his thick, sun-baked arms to stretch, releasing a sour-sweet blend of deodorant and sweat into the salty air. His legs were incongruous to his bloated torso—chunky yet hairless, with powerful calves as hard as marble, the muscles flexing beneath the skin with each lazy shift of his weight. Beads of sweat traced slow, deliberate rivulets down his chest, collecting at his belly before rolling off his sides, their paths etched in the grime of a long, sun-soaked day. The droplets caught the sunlight like lurid jewels, each one marking the passage of time as it dripped onto the hot deck below.

Despite the grotesque display, there was an imposing quality to the man—a hulking, unapologetic presence that radiated dominance, like a beast at rest, aware of its place at the top of the food chain.

"De Paoli," the Captain called, voice thick as oil, so sweet and menacing it made Carlo's skin crawl. His stomach knotted into a hard fist. The pen hovered above the notebook. "Come up here. You look like you could use some sun on that ghostly skin."

Carlo forced himself to meet that voracious

leer, bile rising in his throat. He swallowed, voice shaking. "I—thank you, Captain, but I have work to—"

Garofalo surged to his feet with a deliberate, predatory grace, muscles rippling beneath the glistening sheen of sweat like coiled serpents. "Don't be shy," he purred, his voice slicing through the air like lacquered steel. His thick, powerful hand traced the robust contour of his thigh, tugging aggressively at the speedo's edge in a brazen, obscene invitation. "Show everyone you're not too soft to enjoy a day like today."

Carlo's limbs trembled with revulsion and panic. "I really must—" he began, voice cracking.

"As you wish," Garofalo shrugged, sinking back with a casual disdain that carried an unspoken threat. "But don't say I didn't offer. Wouldn't want you burning out, now, would we?" His laughter rolled across the deck, low and triumphant.

Carlo stumbled back, each retreating footstep echoing like a tolling bell. Behind him, the Captain's laughter trailed through the steel girders like a banner of defeat. On the far corner of the wing, Carlo paused, chest heaving, lungs aflame with heat and humiliation. In that moment of raw clarity, he understood he was ensnared in Garofalo's merciless game—deft, unwinnable, designed to erode him utterly. The ship pressed onward, the unending sea stretching before them, horizonless, indifferent, a vast expanse with no refuge in sight.

~

Later that evening, Carlo perched on the precarious edge of his bunk, with his heart pounding in his ears like the relentless beat of war drums, each throb echoing against the thin metal shell of the cabin. The walls seemed to teeter inward with each laboured breath, the corrugated iron buckling under the weight of the stifling, recycled air, and the pungent smell of engine grease. He pressed his trembling palms flat against his thighs, attempting to suppress the tumult of revulsion and fear that had plagued him since the Captain's *invitation*. The image of Garofalo in that tight, burgundy Speedo—sunlight glinting on bronzed skin, the fabric clinging obscenely to the rounded curves of his buttocks and the prominent bulge of his manhood—flickered behind Carlo's eyelids like a grotesque slideshow. Each replay sent a wave of nausea crashing through him, confirming the grim reality of what he had witnessed. His mind teetered on the precipice of unravelling, a razor's edge of sanity slicing through his thoughts. Desperate for respite, Carlo sought refuge in the cramped shower stall. He let the scalding water batter his shoulders, praying the deluge would wash away the sticky film of shame that clung to him. Instead, the heat drove the ache deeper, as if the steam itself infiltrated his muscles and flayed him from within. With his hair plastered to his forehead like wet seaweed, he found no solace. Steam billowed around him in thick, choking clouds until every vestige of strength seemed sapped away. When he returned to his berth, the familiar hum of the engines had morphed into a piercing whistle lodged inside his skull, an incessant torment that made him wince at each phantom note.

Then came the thump.

A single, deliberate rap that shattered the fragile silence and sent a chill spiraling down his spine. He knew, without turning the latch, who awaited him. As the door creaked open, Captain Garofalo stood framed in the narrow corridor, balanced on a footstool beneath the low ceiling. This time he wore ordinary clothes, though his presence was no less imposing. With a languid motion, he reached up and unscrewed a dead bulb, letting it clink into his palm. His lips curved into a predatory grin in the half-light, a smile that promised nothing but malice.

"Oh, Carlo—just the person I needed," he purred, his voice smooth as silk yet cold as ice. Carlo felt a sharp tightening in his chest, as if his lungs might give way. Garofalo was standing on a small step, trying to replace the light bulb in front of Carlo's cabin. Dressed in just a t-shirt and cargo shorts, he appeared like any ordinary person, the kind who would climb a step, take apart the light bulb fixture, and then realize he had left the new bulb in the toolbox at his feet and out of reach. Without a word, Carlo crawled over the threshold to retrieve the toolbox Garofalo had left on the deck. Kneeling, he rummaged through spanners, spare fuses, and loose screws clicking metallically. His hands trembled so much that the toolbox shook beneath him. Then, there was the unsettling sound of fabric slipping to the floor.

Carlo froze, nerves ablaze. He dared not turn his head—but dread compelled him forward against his will. Slowly, agonizingly, he lifted his gaze. There, at his feet, lay Garofalo's shorts, crumpled around his ankles like a grotesque stage prop. The Captain's buttocks, sagging and peppered with coarse hairs, were bathed in the corridor's harsh glow. Beneath the dark curls, Carlo glimpsed the pale, wrinkled sac of his scrotum and the thick, veined shaft of his penis, in its deliberate, vulgar display of power.

"Oops!" Garofalo laughed, a low, amused rumble that vibrated through Carlo's bones. He remained motionless, savouring the tremor in Carlo's eyes. His dark gaze held Carlo captive—hungry, satisfied.

Carlo's face burned with a shame and fury so intense it felt molten. His throat constricted as he fought the urge to scream or bolt, but the corridor's walls pressed in like an iron trap. The Captain bent at the waist, fingers curling around the waistband of his shorts. With deliberate slowness, he drew them back up, the fabric sliding over skin like a serpent uncoiling. His grin widened, teeth flashing metallically in the dim hall.

"How clumsy." he teased, his voice syrupy and cruel. Then, without another glance at Carlo, he fixed the new bulb into the socket and flicked the switch as if nothing untoward had occurred.

Clutching the toolbox, Carlo felt the world collapse into a single point of humiliation. He managed a nod, backed away, and spoke only in a barely audible whisper. The sting of disgrace scorched him like acid; a wound no water could soothe. When Garofalo hopped down from the stool and strode off—each booted step thudding ominously on the deck plates— Carlo closed the door with a click that resonated like the seal on a coffin.

He sank onto his bunk, the cabin felt smaller now—walls bending inward, the steady thrum of the ship transformed into a giant's pulse reminding him he was trapped. He hugged himself, seeking shelter from the rawness within. Anger welled up like a furnace's blaze, urging him to strike, to scream, to break something—but fear, cold and unyielding, held him paralyzed, whispering that any resistance would only deepen his torment.

Night stretched on without mercy. Carlo lay rigid in the oppressive cabin, eyes locked on the riveted ceiling as the ship groaned and trembled around him. Every creak in the bulkhead sounded like an approaching footstep; each shudder of the engines promised further torment. He saw Garofalo's smug face hover in his mind's eye and felt violated anew. No physical blow had been struck, but the psychological assault gouged deeper than any bruise. As exhaustion drifted over him like a distant fog, Carlo understood with chilling clarity that this had never been about a lightbulb or a harmless prank. It was a sick contest of power—and the Captain was only just beginning to play.

Helpless and alone, Carlo feared how far the game would extend next.

~

Carlo had watched Garofalo's demeanour warp over the course of several weeks, like a photograph left too long in the sun. At first there'd been a mere tremor in the Captain's polite reserve—a hesitation in his eyes, the briefest shadow crossing his lips. Then gradually, imperceptibly, that tremor became a fissure, and the fissure widened into a yawning crack of unpredictability and menace. Whenever they were alone, Garofalo's practiced, gentle charm would peel away as though it were a thin mask, revealing beneath it a pair of eyes that measured Carlo with cold, analytical precision.

What had once been a reassuring pat on the shoulder lingered now, fingertips clawing into flesh, a silent promise that no part of the ship—no place, no person—was ever truly out of his reach. Carlo felt the walls of the vessel close in on him. He could almost hear his own heartbeat hammering behind his ribs, a coil of panic tightening in his gut with every passing evening. He knew the pattern: first one man, then another. Late at night, when the ship creaked and sighed, hushed rumours would carry through the bulkheads—whispered tales of boundaries crossed, of shame so absolute it rendered victims voiceless, of *accidental* contact so bruising it left bodies and souls battered. And among all the crew, Mateo was by far Garofalo's most vulnerable quarry. A quiet Filipino steward born on a weather-worn island so small it barely registered on navigational charts; Mateo had always been the embodiment of gentleness. His hands, calloused by years of washing dishes and scrubbing galley floors, moved with a careful grace whenever he tended to linens or polished the Captain's shoes. Each dollar he sent back to his family was a lifeline to a fragile ladder out of generational poverty. Every month away from home was agony and salvation bound together: the ache for missing his children's laughter, the pride in sustaining them. In Garofalo's cabin, Mateo scuttled like a shadow, his posture so humble you might almost miss him. That illusion shattered one humid morning. Mateo had just smoothed the last fold of freshly laundered sheets, his back stiff with repeated motions, when the snap of the shower valve reached his ears. The bathroom door swung open, steam billowing into the room like a theatrical fog, and there stood Garofalo: water still coursing down his broad, bulky torso. The towel wrapped around his waist slipped free in a deliberate, ominous arc that left Mateo's face flushing with shame before panic could take hold. He wanted to look away, to curse his own curiosity, but his gaze was locked, helpless.

In an instant, Garofalo closed the distance. His long shadow swallowed the steward as he reached out, fingers like iron bands clamping around Mateo's throat. The younger man's knees buckled, his world narrowing to the rasp of his own rapid breathing, the pressure suffocating him. Eyes stinging, chest heaving, he tasted the copper tang of fear. Garofalo's voice, low and hoarse with perverse satisfaction, slithered into his ear: "Good stewards know how to serve." With his free hand, the Captain moved over Mateo's body, each contact dragging across him like barbed wire, erasing any claim the steward had to safety or dignity. Pure terror ripped through Mateo, and though his mind screamed for escape, his limbs trembled too violently to obey. He could only press his back into the starched linens he himself had fluffed and tucked, sobbing silently as his tears salted his own shirt. He saw, in that moment of utter helplessness, the faces of his little ones—bright eyes full of trust, small hands waving goodbye at dawn. Their images flickered like candle flames in a draft. But the real world weighed him down: the Captain's body pinned him, the assault crushing his spirit beneath its brutal weight. His tears came in hot, shame-soaked rivers, but his voice remained paralyzed by the twin chains of fear and humiliation.

Far below the deck lights that glowed like fallen stars, Carlo lay awake in his narrow bunk. In the darkness behind his closed eyelids, he replayed Mateo's horror in the same agonizing details his crewmates had disclosed to him.

At length, unable to endure the guilt any longer, he slipped from his berth and crept through the passageways until he found himself in the paint storeroom, as he let the tears come—hot, merciless tears that bore down on his chest like stones. He cursed himself for abandoning his own home, for believing that the open sea might offer freedom rather than this floating prison of steel and predators. There was no heroism here. Only silent cages in which men like Garofalo roamed free and preyed on the weak. Time slipped away as Carlo's thoughts drifted to his family—his mother scrubbing salt-crusted nets, his father's sun-weathered, stern face, and his cousins' distant shouts from the stone docks where generations had fished. In a community where deep-sea sailing was the pinnacle of honour, shame weighed heavier than death. If he chose to leave the ship of his own accord, what rumours would reach his island's rocky shores? That Carlo had forsaken his responsibilities, that he had failed to uphold the proud tradition of his sailor lineage. His mother would have to avert her eyes in the marketplace, and his father's reputation would be stained by his son's perceived cowardice. It would be a betrayal of everything they had ever known.

The thought of slipping over the rail into the ocean's endless darkness felt less like a horror and more like an escape—an exile from the very core of the world he had desperately tried to leave behind.

He found himself at the rail, knuckles tightening as he gripped the rusted metal, the cold night wind biting at his face. Beneath him, the ocean stretched into an abyss darker than despair itself. He closed his eyes and leaned forward, ready to surrender—to feel the sea's final embrace.

Then came the alarms. They exploded into the night like a barrage of gunfire: shrill, relentless. "Man overboard! Man overboard!" The warning thundered from the speakers, ricocheting violently off bulkheads and hatches. The ship's CCTV had last captured Carlo's shadow looming over the rail, and an officer, discovering his cabin empty, had sounded the alarm. Now the crew erupted across the decks, hurling life rings into the sea, voices shouting his name, convinced they were in a frantic race to save a drowning man. Footsteps pounded onto the deck, searchlights pierced the darkness, wild as desperate eyes hunting prey. They did not know that the man they pursued was not in the water, but there, trapped in a nightmare that would persist as long as his contract lasted. Carlo's entire body spasmed violently, his heart leaping with wild confusion. He had not jumped. A tumult of relief and fear twisted inside him—relief that he was still alive, fear that he remained a captive.

~

"Come here," Garofalo's voice was unwavering—a low, predatory growl that pressed against Carlo's spine. Carlo's chest constricted. Ahead, the Captain leaned against the forward bulkhead with a lazy confidence, one shoulder propped, the other hand buried deep in his trouser pocket. The sour tang of stale coffee clung to him. Carlo could almost taste the bitterness on his tongue, feel its heat at his temples.

"You're a good worker," Garofalo purred, the words rumbling in his throat like distant thunder. Carlo should have felt honoured—flattered even—but the compliment landed like bait on a hook. The Captain straightened, stepping forward until his hot breath ghosted over Carlo's collarbone. "Potential shines in you." Carlo swallowed hard. He had poured every ounce of himself into this ship. And yet that single ominous syllable—*but*—loomed between them, an unspoken promise of pain. He didn't have to wait long. Garofalo's lips curled into a cruel smile. "But that hissy fit you threw last night—completely unacceptable." The sweet sheen of praise soured in Carlo's ears. "We're men here. We settle matters like men. *Capisce*?"

A tremor ran through Carlo's limbs. Now, with Garofalo's dark eyes fixed on him, Carlo would have given anything to keep his job. He clenched his fists and nodded wordlessly.

"What were you thinking?" Garofalo said in a change of tone, surprisingly fatherly. "Let's talk, Carlo" the Captain mused, it was the first time he had ever called him by his first name. His voice lowered "You've done such good work, you've performed well above anyone else..." —a hope, a glimpse of understanding, finally the lesson from all that hardship would come to make sense— "But I know you can give me more." He reached out, fingertips ghosting over Carlo's forearm in a calculated gesture. Carlo flinched, muscles coiling, shattered. "You and I...we have an understanding, don't we? We can make this work, like a trade." Each word dropped like a corrosive drop of acid.

Carlo strained for composure. "Sir, I just want to focus on my job." His voice was a brittle whisper. Garofalo's grip tightened around Carlo's arm, bones pressing painfully through the fabric. "You respect me, don't you?" he hissed, leaning in close enough that Carlo could feel the Captain's heartbeat thundering through his chest. "Show me how much." The world seemed to whirl around Carlo as his knees threatened to give way, leaving him teetering on the brink of collapse. The captain's hand moved toward Carlo's shoulder, exerting a downward pressure. It was a gesture inviting Carlo to succumb to the degrading obedience he had resisted so far. For a fleeting moment, he considered that giving in to the captain's depravity might be his only chance to endure another day. Even then, he summoned all his remaining defiance and managed to utter a shaky affirmation: "I—I respect you, Captain. Let me demonstrate it through my work." The Captain chuckled—a low, mocking sound. He released Carlo with a deliberate slowness, stroking his hand along the doorframe before leaning back into the shadows. "For now, you're free to go. But remember...you'll come around." With that parting promise, he vanished, leaving Carlo's, senses screaming.

Before dawn, the vessel slipped into Bangkok's crowded container terminal. The heavy, humid air clung to every surface, redolent with salt, oil, and rust. High pressure water jets hissed as the mooring lines shot ashore, their drenched coils snapping against the bollards. The third officer shouted orders while Carlo, just off duty from the forward mooring deck, wiped sweat from his brow and hurried toward his quarters. At the gangway he spotted a familiar stevedore, surly, cigarette-stained fingers betraying years of tobacco use—known for doing favours at a price. In a hushed, rapid exchange, Carlo arranged to have his rolled-up belongings smuggled ashore later that day amid a jumble of wooden crates.

The night before, Carlo had waited until the ship settled into the stillness of midnight. Under the fluorescent glare of the control room, he accessed the discharge form template on the computer. He forged the necessary paperwork, typing his name in neat, steady letters—leaving captain's signature line blank.

As first light crept over the city, the main deck exploded into motion. Dockworkers swarmed the pier, port officials in sweat-spotted white uniforms boarded armed with thick binders of customs and immigration forms. The captain took his place in the control room, barking orders as he juggled demands from port authorities, stevedores, and impatient officers.

Carlo seized the moment. He slipped his forged discharge papers into the stack awaiting the captain's signature. Garofalo barely glanced up as he picked up the top form, pen scratching across the page with the careless efficiency of a man who never reads the fine print. Carlo held his breath, then eased the signed sheet into his chest pocket, and backed away. Moments later, carrying a bag weighed down with his belongings, Carlo strode toward the gangway. The deckhands, half-awake and half-distracted, scarcely registered his passing.

~

Outside on deck, the humid air of Bangkok enveloped him in a heavy, steamy atmosphere woven with the roar of taxis, the clang of street vendors, the swirl of spices and incense. For the first time in months, he let himself breathe. As dawn painted the horizon red, Carlo sat on a low wooden bench by the quay. The MV Lawrence loomed in the distance, its massive form cutting a stark figure against the brightening sky. Carlo observed as the engines revved up and the ship began to move slowly away from the dock, taking with it the presence of Garofalo. With each meter of water that spread between them, Carlo felt his months of suffering dissipate, like chains being undone one by one. He imagined the chaos and anger Garofalo would experience upon realizing he had unwittingly authorized the escape of his target. Carlo pondered who Garofalo might have chosen as his next victim. He closed his eyes to the rising sun, drew in the thick, fragrant air, and let hope seep into the hollows that fear had carved. The memory of those days would mark him for years to come. But on this solid ground, bathed in Bangkok's clammy embrace, Carlo dared to believe in something more than survival. He had escaped. And in that truth lay the first, fragile bloom of peace.

~

Carlo never set foot in his hometown again after he slipped away from the creaking planks of that merchant ship. In his mind, the sun-drenched lanes lined with gnarled olive trees and whitewashed cottages had become as insubstantial as the clouds that drifted across the sky—too fragile to hold onto, too far away to touch.

Carlo had learnt that geography meant nothing when the pain lived inside you. He'd endured storms that shrieked through his very core, and he'd obeyed Garofalo's ruthless orders in the rusty holds of the MV Lawrence. The boy who once roamed vine-draped walls, racing through sunlit courtyards, had been ground down until only a hollow shell remained.

To go home, to become that boy again, filled him with a sense of terror so deep he felt it clench at his ribs.

So, he set out on a journey without maps or timetables, carrying only a battered duffel bag and a heart desperate to beat its own rhythm. He crossed borders like a restless breeze, from continent to continent, chasing dawns that broke in golden light over alien rooftops.

Everywhere he went, the wind found him—rattling his clothes, tugging at his hair, reminding him that he answered to no one but himself. Carlo meandered through the winding alleys of ancient medinas, enveloped by the rich aroma of spices and incense. He traversed deserts where the wind murmured secrets through ever-changing dunes and swam in lagoons so clear they seemed to wash away the burdens of his past. In the distant north, he navigated icy fjords, the frigid glacier-fed waters biting against his skin, and watched the aurora borealis dance in silent rapture.

With every new dawn, he felt his spirit gradually mend. Beyond the rigid confines of the MV Lawrence, he rediscovered the sensation of true freedom—unrestrained, unanchored, and fully alive.

Every sunrise brought back a warmth he once believed gone for good. He remembered the cramped alleys of his village, where every glance felt like judgment, and the weight of expectations bore down on him. Garofalo's ship was no better, like an iron cage that twisted his sense of self. Under a sky he didn't know, with the horizon stretching endlessly, he sensed the whispers of freedom. He realized that freedom didn't mean reverting to his past self, which had been shattered by trauma and overshadowed by self-doubt. Though bent, he was not broken, and he moved forward, with his scars standing as proof of survival. With each breath of salty air, his spirit began to heal.

~

After years of travels, Carlo found himself drawn to a rugged Scottish shore where cliffs met the ocean and hills rose like sleeping giants. The air was a mix of sandstone, gorse, and heather. Narrow paths traced the jagged coastline, worn smooth by tides and footsteps. Waves crashed against volcanic rocks, sending sprays into the dim, grey light. A decaying stone pier reached into turbulent waters, its surface polished by fishermen and storms.

Above, a medieval fortress clung to a rocky outcrop, its walls marked by sea salt and overgrown with vines.

Carlo rented a modest room in a stone cottage on a windswept hill, its walls streaked with salt and grit. From his small window, he watched the tide reveal and conceal jagged reefs like a sunken monster's ribs. In the morning, he would walk the coastal path, with the North Sea's chill wind tingling his cheeks. Despite its roughness, the place offered a quiet welcome—a chance to blend into its rhythm without question.

What was intended as a brief break stretched into weeks, then months. Carlo found steady work in the small shipyard behind the promenade, repairing wooden hulls scarred by years at sea. His hands remembered the grain of oak planks, the resistance of caulk under pressure, the ring of metal against wood as he drove clamps into place. With each fresh coat of varnish, with each careful seal of a keel, he felt strength return—quiet, honest strength born of artisanry, far from cruel commands and steel chains.

It was on a brisk autumn morning—when the

air smelled of seaweed and woodsmoke, and the first dead leaves skittered across the cobblestones—that Carlo's life would shift once more, in a way he could never have anticipated.

~

The first grey fingers of dawn stretched hesitantly across the water, painting the horizon in gentle shades of pearl and lavender, as Carlo lifted his booted foot onto the salt-worn timbers of the old harbour pier. Tiny droplets of mist clung to the ropes coiled at his feet, and in the dim light the heavy wooden crates stacked along the quay looked as though they might topple at the slightest breath of wind. Nets lay draped over barrels and beams, their fine mesh glimmering like cobwebs in the soft glow, as if some giant spider had spun them overnight. Beyond the edge of the pier the town lay wrapped in a diaphanous curtain of morning fog, its cobblestones slick and shining. The only sounds were the distant cries of seagulls wheeling overhead—sharp, ragged keens—and the measured slap of waves against the pylons.

All at once, that fragile calm splintered. The wail of a siren cut through the dawn's hush like a blade, shrill and unyielding, ripping Carlo from his reverie. He dropped the coil of fishing line he had been inspecting and, without pausing to question the urgency in his chest, raced toward the narrow path that led up the slope behind the quay. Above him, the sky was pale, but he saw a plume of dense, inky smoke unfurling into the air, twisting like a restless beast eager to devour the heavens. His heart hammered against his ribs as he scrambled over rough stones, driven by a need to see, to help—though he had no idea what awaited him.

Carlo halted, utterly breathless, before a venerable stone dwelling that had stood for generations now rent open by ferocious orange flames. The fire roared like a hungry animal, its tongue-shaped bursts licking at the blackened parapets and sending showers of glowing

225

embers spiralling upward into the cool morning air. Windows had shattered, a team of firefighters advanced steadily under a sky streaked with smoke. The hiss and steam of water meeting flame punctuated their focused shouts, and every so often a droplet of boiling spray snapped on impact, adding a sibilant hiss to the cacophony. A small crowd of onlookers gathered at a safe distance, their faces pale and anxious, whispers of disbelief drifting on the smoke-choked breeze.

Carlo forced himself forward through the cluster of townspeople, compelled by some deep impulse he could neither name nor resist. It was there, just beyond the perimeter of the firefighters' cordon, that he saw the boy—a child no older than eight—standing alone, his posture stiff with horror. The child's clothes were singed at the hems, and tufts of hair clung in dark, ashen clumps to his forehead. Dirt and soot streaked his cheeks, tracing thin, trembling lines beneath bright, terrified eyes. Carlo recognized the grief: stunned, hollow, wordless. He had lost to water; the boy, to fire. He knelt on the rough stone edge of a collapsed garden wall, the coarse surface pressing uncomfortably against his denim trousers, and held out his hand in a gesture at once simple and profound.

He lowered his voice until it was nearly drowned by the roar of water and flame. "What's your name?" he asked gently. The boy's reply was almost a whisper: "Angus," he said, his voice hoarse and small. "Angus," Carlo repeated, as if tasting the name, offering a gentle nod and the faintest lift of his lips. "I'm Carlo."

In the days that followed, the townspeople spoke in low tones of the tragedy—a family consumed by fire, a small boy left alone in the world. Carlo found himself unable to shake the image of Angus, trembling and alone, his small form framed by the smoke-blackened ruins. He had no clear plan, no rational reason for what he did next, but something ancient and unyielding seemed to guide him—a force born of his own years at sea, where decisions had to be made in the face of chaos without time for second guessing.

He had approached the local authorities, unsure of what he hoped to achieve. The boy had no remaining family, at least none who had

come forward, and the town's modest re-
sources meant Angus would likely be sent
away, his fate decided by strangers in a distant, faceless office. The thought gnawed at
Carlo, who had once felt the same bitter helplessness when his own world had collapsed.
The parish priest who looked after the boy and
who had known Carlo since his early days in
the village, listened quietly as Carlo stumbled
through his reasoning. "You don't have to
make it permanent," Carlo said gently. "That
child just needs a safe place to land. I could be
that place—just until we know more."

That night, Carlo lay awake in his cottage, listening to the waves batter the rocks outside.
He couldn't sleep—partly hanging in the balance of an outcome he was so powerless upon,
partly because he wasn't sure how to care for a
child who had lost everything. Yet, when he
thought about Angus, alone and frightened,
the choice seemed less like a decision and
more like a calling.
The next morning, Carlo returned to the priest
who had agreed to let him take Angus in, at
least for the time being. When he brought the
boy to his small cottage at the water's edge,

Angus clung to his side, unsure of what to expect. As the tide whispered against the rocks, Carlo knelt down and met Angus's gaze. "You don't have to be scared," he said, his voice softer than he'd intended. "We'll take it one day at a time."

For the first time since the fire, Angus didn't look away. He nodded—a small, hesitant motion—and then, to Carlo's surprise, reached for his hand. Carlo held it, the small fingers cool against his calloused palm and felt something shift inside him—a sense of purpose, fragile but real, like the first stirrings of spring after a long, bitter winter.

In the first weeks, Angus moved through the cottage like a shadow. He slipped from room to room with caution. Carlo never pressured him to speak of his feelings; instead, he wove gentle routines around the boy's fragile world. Together, before first light, they repaired frayed fishing nets. In the pale evenings, they wandered among tidepools, marvelling at barnacles clinging like clusters of tiny stars and anemones pulsing with life. Week after week, they strolled through the market, inhaling the briny scent of fresh fish mingled with the sweet tang of tomatoes and citrus.

Sometimes, they claimed a favoured spot on the slope that overlooked the sea, where the sky bled into the horizon in molten hues of coral and gold. Angus, once a trembling boy, would sit with knees drawn up, tracing patterns in the sand with a slender stick. Carlo watched the slow transformation in him: the way his shoulders relaxed, how the panic in his dark eyes gave way to quiet reflection. In these shared silences, Carlo felt an unexpected tenderness blooming within him—a fierce protectiveness, a deep longing to shield the boy from every sorrow the world could summon. He knew too well what it meant to face the world unguarded.

Even as the seasons changed and the boy returned to school Angus remained an outsider—a slender, pale figure with dark hair blowing in the cool wind. His frame was too slight for his age, and his eyes seemed too wise for his years. Despite the change of scenery, the new town reflected the same social dynamics as Carlo's past: a close-knit community wary of outsiders and harsh toward anyone different. As an orphaned outsider resistant to conformity, Angus quickly learned to navigate a world where his uniqueness set him apart. Carlo saw the familiar signs—the silent glares, the whispered insults—mirroring the social challenges he had once faced but never truly confronted. He had left his island without ever returning. Maybe that's why he tried to impart the only lessons he knew, taking Angus fishing on Sundays or exploring tide pools in search of crabs and polished glass. But Angus was always a solitary soul, clutching his children's encyclopaedias—dog-eared and worn, filled with detailed drawings and maps. These books offered him a world he could explore alone, where every question had a clear answer, unlike the chaotic nature of human relationships. Carlo would glance at the boy, his dark head bent over the pages, small fingers tracing paths of ancient explorers and forgotten rivers and feel a pang of recognition.

As months turned to years, Carlo could no longer ignore the mirror his new companion held up to him. He, too, had learned to endure, to stand firm against storms and adversity. He saw that same flicker of resilience in Angus: a stubborn spark hidden beneath layers of grief. One afternoon, with gulls wheeling overhead and sunlight dancing on the breakers, Carlo paused in their stroll along a shoreline strewn with bleached driftwood and tangled seaweed. He looked down at the boy, noting the steadier gait, the curious tilt of his head as he examined a worn piece of amber glass.

"You remind me of someone I knew a long time ago," Carlo said slowly, his voice soft and distant, as though speaking across an ocean of memory. "Someone who had to grow up too fast." Angus stopped and looked up; his eyes bright with curiosity. "Who?"

Carlo gave a small, rueful smile that creased the corners of his weathered eyes. "Me." And in that simple confession lay years of longing, regret, and hope.

Life in the town continued its familiar patterns, but something fundamental had shifted in Carlo's world and in Angus's. The boy spent less time at the window, more time by Carlo's side—in the summers he would help at the shipyard, asking questions about the tides and the calls of certain seabirds. When Carlo teased him about the telltale trail of sand he left from yard to hearth, a shy grin would break across Angus's face, and Carlo's heart swelled with an unfamiliar joy. But the world beyond their cottage was not always kind. Back at school, Angus's quietness, and the scars faintly visible on his arms made him a target. He returned home one afternoon with bruises flaring through the fabric of his sleeves, and Carlo, recognizing the pain of such cruelty, felt anger rise in his chest. He did not respond with anger of his own—forged threats or harsh lectures—but with stories. He told Angus of nights when waves had towered over the deck, when men had quarrelled in the darkness, and he had wrestled not just the sea but despair itself. And in the afternoons, as they sat on the shore while the tide inched in, Carlo's gravelly voice wove lessons of resilience into the steady pulse of the surf, reminding the boy that true strength was not the absence of fear but the courage to face it. "When I was a boy," Carlo began, his voice rough but steady, as he worked the buttons of Angus's shirt with slow, careful fingers, "we had a dog named Kunak. Big, muscular beast. Could've cleared the garden wall without a thought... but he never did." Angus sniffled, his tear-filled eyes fixed on the floor, his small shoulders rigid with protest beneath Carlo's hands. He didn't want to go back to school — not after what they'd done to him yesterday. Carlo's hands lingered for a moment, steady and quiet, before he spoke again. "See, when Kunak was a pup, my father kept him chained in the yard. Heavy iron links, thick enough to hold back a bear. But as he grew, the chain was replaced with lighter ropes... eventually, just an old piece of twine." He paused, smoothing the fabric near Angus's collar. "But Kunak never tested it. Never tried to run. He'd learned his limits so well, he carried them even when they weren't real anymore."

Carlo crouched slightly, his voice softening, as though letting Angus in on a quiet secret. "That's what happens sometimes when you grow up somewhere that tells you what you're allowed to be. You carry the weight of that chain long after it's gone... forgetting you're free to go as far as you dare."

Angus stayed quiet, knuckling a tear from his cheek. "One day," Carlo finished, buttoning the last button gently, "you'll leave this place.

And when you do, you'll get to decide if you want to keep that rope around your neck... or break it. The world's bigger than they've made you believe... and you're stronger than you know.

No story could undo what the fire had taken: Angus's home, the three storey, sandstone and granite marvel that had been their town's beating heart. His parents—an architect who saw walls as hidden doors and a lawyer who turned wild designs into iron-clad contracts—had built the country's first multi-storey escape-room house. Each room brimmed with sliding panels, false floors, rotating bookcases, cipher wheels, and secret passages spiralling to a glass-domed observatory overlooking the sea. They had met at a conference, bonding over riddles and drafting their first escape-room blueprint on a cocktail napkin in a hotel bar. Back home, they shored up an old stone building with creaking beams, transforming every corner into a living puzzle. Guests laughed and whispered clues among walls that themselves whispered back.

Now only a charred shell remained—windows like lifeless eyes, staircases collapsed into ash, gears rusted, puzzle pieces scattered. The fire had silenced the laughter, erased the hidden mechanisms, and scattered decades of secrets into blackened dust.

One evening, as the sun sank in a blaze of molten gold, Carlo spotted Angus standing before the boarded-up ruins, sealed off since the fire all those years ago, his young face pale in the fading light. The boy's eyes, usually so quick to wander in wonder, were fixed on the crumbling walls. Carlo felt a gentle stirring of hope and spoke the words he had carried in his heart.

"What if we rebuilt your house?" he asked softly.

Angus turned, his eyes widening. "Rebuild it?" His voice trembled on the question, as though daring to believe.

"Not just rebuild," Carlo replied. "We'll transform it into a museum—a living tribute to your parents' creation. An escape room museum, where people can come and discover every secret passage and hidden door, just as they did before."

For a long, breathless moment, the boy stood silent, as though weighing the possibility.

Then, slowly, a single nod quivered through him. "A museum... like the escape rooms?" he whispered.

"Exactly," Carlo confirmed, warmth flooding him. "You know every trick and trap. You can help design it, room by room, puzzle by puzzle. We will build it together."

And so, armed with hammers and chisels, fresh mortar and bristles of dust, Carlo and Angus embarked on a new journey. Each weekend they laboured among twisted iron and mounds of ash, sorting through salvageable stone and cataloguing battered fragments of wood. By the light of lanterns, they spread yellowed blueprints across a workbench, pencils scratching as Angus reimagined secret doors and trapdoors, each sketch a spark of his parents' ingenuity reborn. Carlo watched the boy's eyes shine with purpose, felt warmth unfurl in his chest as each restored brick and fashioned mechanism brought them closer to something whole once more.

As the years passed, the house took shape around them, its walls rising like the slow unfurling of a new beginning. Angus grew taller, his once thin frame filling out as he took on more of the demanding physical work. He learned to repair locks, oil rusted hinges, and polish the worn floorboards until they gleamed under the flicker of gaslight. After school, he could often be found sweeping the tiled halls or adjusting the ropes and pulleys that operated the museum's hidden mechanisms, his dark eyes narrowing in concentration as he tested each mechanism with a craftsman's precision. He moved through the house like a ghost-turned-caretaker, his small, pale hands stained with the dust of ancient stones and the ink of freshly drawn sketches, his once timid silhouette now a familiar shadow among the restored corridors.

In rebuilding the house, they rebuilt themselves. And with every echoing strike of hammer on chisel, every careful layer of mortar, they laid the foundations not only of a museum, but of a shared life born of loss, bound by hope, and defined by resilience.

~

As the years unfurled like the turning pages of a grand, leather tome, the old manor underwent a transformation so gradual and thorough it felt as though time itself had taken up a paintbrush. Where once the bricks lay smudged with soot and streaked by centuries of rain, now a fresh coat of ochre warmed the corners of every archway, and swaths of creamy white trimmed each window as though the house wore a fine collar. Craftsmen's hammers tapped in measured rhythms, joiners smoothed new bannisters into honeyed wood, and painters moved ladders in whispered procession along the walls. As he grew well into his teenage years, Angus, stepping carefully from one foyer into the next, could navigate the manor blindfolded: he felt beneath his fingertips the carved grooves of an iron grate hidden behind a secret panel in the library; he knew where to press a weathered bust just so to release the latch; he remembered the vertiginous spiral chute that deposited amused guests into a hidden chamber, their shrieks of surprise still ringing in his ears. In every clink of metal, every rumble of a sliding stone, Angus recognized the legacy of his parents' dream—and the evolving contours of his own. But as the museum flourished under their joint stewardship, time pressed its own demands upon Carlo's body. The brilliant grin that once lit every room now came attached to a fine tremor in his fingers, as if the centuries-old gears he had tended were finally wearing thin. Mornings greeted him with stiff joints that sighed beneath each step and a cough—first hesitant, then growing into a rasp that cut through conversations.

Evening after evening, he lingered too long beside display cabinets, his palm sliding over glass as though tracing the life stories encased within. Angus watched those weary shoulders, marked by sighs, and the tremulous pause Carlo took at every bench, his great love for the manor failing to mask the burden it now posed. It pained Angus more than he could say to see the man whose hands had built wonders begin to falter under their weight.

One evening, after the last guests had drifted out into the cool night and the iron lanterns in the great hall guttered low, Angus found Carlo leaning against an alabaster column, its pale surface glowing in the flicker of the single remaining flame. Carlo's shoulders slumped as though he had carried invisible stones for decades, and in that moment, he looked diminished—no longer the towering figure of Angus's youth, but a man who had finally set down his burdens.

"Papa," Angus said, voice firm but soft with affection, "we can't keep doing this to you."

Carlo's tired eyes met his, pride and resignation passing between them.

Carlo and Angus had moved into the attic of the very house they had resurrected—a modest space beneath creaking rafters and sloping beams, where the walls still held the warmth of summer and the floors echoed with the softened laughter of guests below.

By day, the museum bustled with the clatter of footsteps and the low murmur of riddles. Journalists and tourists came from across the country to marvel at the house that had risen from its own ruin, drawn by tales of endurance and renewal. Up in the attic, however, a different life unfolded—quieter, simpler, marked by the soft scratch of Angus's pencil as he sketched new designs, the rustle of old blueprints, and the steady, comforting thrum of the sea beyond the thin, salt-streaked windows.

There they shared late suppers at a small wooden table, their shadows long against the slanted walls, conversation softened by the attic's warm air. On balmy nights, they pushed the windows open to let in the cool breeze carrying the distant murmur of waves. And though the grand house below continued to whisper its secrets to those brave enough to listen, Carlo and Angus found a new peace high above it all—a peace born not of silence, but of the gentle, ceaseless murmur of lives rebuilt.

One evening, as Carlo lowered himself into his chair at the dinner table, he winced but waved off Angus's concerned hand. The lamp cast long shadows across his silver hair, illuminating each thread with an amber glow. He managed a gentle smile, though his chest rose with the effort of the breath. "You've always been a blessing to me," he murmured, his voice soft as velvet but carrying the weight of countless unspoken feelings. Angus paused, a spoon halfway to his mouth, brow knitting in tender confusion. "A blessing?" he echoed, setting the spoon aside as though its steadiness could not rival the gravity of the moment.

Carlo closed his eyes and drew in a long, steady breath that carried with it the scent of every memory he had carefully curated through the years. In his mind's eye, he saw the terrified boy curled beside the hearth in the aftermath of the great fire. He remembered the child who had refused to surrender, who gathered charred fragments of wood and broken panes of glass to rebuild both home and hope. He recalled how that boy's resilience had bloomed into something luminous, a promise etched in courage and ingenuity. Exhaling, Carlo spoke the word in his native language Italian, each syllable a gentle benediction. "In my language — in Italian" he said, his voice painting the word in the air, "we call it *benedizione.*"

Angus slowly savoured the word—*be-ne-di-tsio-ne*—enjoying the smooth vowels and gentle consonants until it settled warmly within him, reminiscent of a long—learned melody.

In that single word, he felt the weight of survival, the glow of shared victories, and the promise of the future. For the first time, he experienced a raw sense of belonging, as if shaped perfectly to fit his slender, teenage form. After a while, his shoulders relaxed, like a hidden mechanism had clicked into place. He looked up at Carlo, his eyes shining in the lamplight. "I like it." Though brief, the word was rich with meaning, unlocking the future. In the comfortable silence that followed, Carlo felt a certainty he had not found in the manor's corridors: he had achieved enough, built enough, and dedicated more than a lifetime's worth. Across the table, Angus sat a bit straighter, as if the gentle strength of the word reinforced him against any upcoming challenges. His eyes danced with the notion of a newfound identity. For Angus, the evening was more than a routine; it was a confirmation that he was no longer just a boy shaped by tragedy, but the creator of his own future. As the amber lamplight softly illuminated their faces, the quiet promise of *benedizione* shone like a guiding light, uniting them in a golden embrace through time.

"Ben," he said softly.

Carlo chuckled—a deep, content sound that blended with the quiet of their simple dining room. "Ben it is, then." he agreed, and in that moment, the new name lingered between them, like a ribbon tying the past and future together.

4.

WIND

"I am a part of all that I have met." —Alfred Tennyson

The island stirred before dawn, as if rousing from a deep, dreamless sleep. A soft moan drifted across the terraced slopes and olive groves, the land yawning beneath its early-morning veil. Gradually, pale bands of pink and violet unfurled along the eastern sky, each hinting at the fierce midday sun to come, yet for now the air remained crisp with seawater and faintly scented by wild thyme on a barely-there breeze. Beyond the terraces, twisted olive trees clung to the rocky ground while rugged, sun-bleached hills tumbled toward the sea like a crumpled sheet of linen. Perched high above narrow coves and jagged inlets, whitewashed locals' cottages hugged the cliffs, their walls etched by salt and countless storms. Below, the water gleamed in shifting shades of sapphire and turquoise, marbled with foam where currents collided over the submerged reefs known as Le Colonne. To the west, where sea met sky in one seamless line, the lighthouse at Capo Sandalo cast its solitary shadow over restless waves. On the island's far side, the flat salt pans lay like polished glass, their shallow pools mirroring dawn's first blush as flocks of pink flamingos dipped graceful necks into the brine.

Above it all, atop the island's highest point, the watchtower of Guardia dei Mori kept silent vigil. Its crumbling walls, stained by centuries of salt and sun, faced the western horizon— forever waiting for the return of some long-lost vessel. From the depths of the narrow, cobbled lanes came the first tentative sounds of day. There was the muffled clamour of loaves of bread being eased from a wooden oven into wicker baskets, the faint rasp of a lone motorbike stirring from its quiet rest, and the gentle tinkle of porcelain cups as sleepy cafés eased open their shutters and greeted the dawn. A solitary gull cried overhead, its keening call bouncing off sun-faded stucco walls, momentarily breaking the hush that clung to the island like dew.

Ben lay awake in his room, the cool plaster ceiling above him shifting in and out of focus between the solidity of waking life and the drifting shapes of dreams. He traced the gentle curves of the hand-painted olive branch motif around the beams of the ceiling, as memories and anticipation danced together in his mind. For years he had carried this island within him—not simply as a name on a map, but as a living echo of Carlo's voice. Carlo had spoken of every hidden cove and gnarled pine tree with such deep affection that Ben could almost taste the salt on his tongue and feel smooth pebbles beneath his bare feet. At last, restless, he rose and crossed the cool ceramic floor to the balcony doors. The sky was now a softly luminous canvas, the lavender heights melting into pale apricot closer to the water. He embraced his freshly-made cappuccino cup from his room's kitchenette and watched the steam weave ghostlike ribbons above the thick crema. The Baia d'Argento Hotel clung to the cliff's edge, its sun-bleached walls blending seamlessly into the ochre stone as though grown from the living rock itself. Far below, the sea lay outstretched in molten sheets of cerulean and silver, each slow, rolling wave brushing the sandy shoreline in a lover's caress.

Ben should have felt a kind of peace in that moment. Instead, his chest tightened as memory pressed in. Carlo's sudden departure had shattered the quiet confidence of everything Ben thought he knew. This man—larger than life, who spoke to winds as old friends, who sang the island's ancient stories into Ben's ear—now existed only in the silver cylinder resting in his backpack. Carlo had left explicit instructions: no marble tomb, no scattering on sterile ground. He wanted a green burial, his flesh returned to the earth, then powdered and released to the sea that first had cradled him.

In his breast pocket lay the folded letter Carlo had entrusted to him—unread since those first trembling hours after his passing. He did not need to open it again; its words had taken root in his heart and blossomed there in a quiet litany of love and farewell. Beneath the folded page, he could still feel the gentle curve of

Carlo's script, the way each letter seemed to pulse with warmth.

As daylight intensified, he placed the empty coffee cup down, shifted the pack on his back, and walked into the sunlit corridor. The path to Mezzaluna Bay stretched out ahead, resembling a silver thread weaving through hills adorned with lush pines and fragrant rosemary. He mounted the bicycle borrowed from the hotel and coasted down the road, surrounded by Mediterranean scrub and its herbal aroma. Cicadas scattered around sang their soft melody, while the sea breeze filled his lungs, bringing the promise of a fresh day. Sunlight filtered through an arch of leaning branches, casting playful dances of light and shadow across the winding path. Each breath he drew was tinged with the brine of the sea and the heady sweetness of juniper blossoms clinging to craggy outcrops. Occasionally, the breeze would pick up, ruffling his hair as though Carlo himself was whispering encouragement in his ear.

By midmorning, he reached the cliffside overlook guarding Mezzaluna Bay. From this height, the water below gleamed with the rich green of polished malachite, lapping gently against a pristine crescent of sand and smooth stones. A ruined stone fort perched above the cove, its ivy-clad walls crumbling at the edges, as though time and tide were coaxing it back to dust. All was hushed here, as if the world had paused in reverence for what was to come.

Ben parked the bike on a patch of sun-warmed earth and shouldered his pack. He picked his way down the narrow, winding trail. At the very edge of the cliff, he knelt on the sun-baked rock. He set his pack beside him and drew out the slim silver cylinder. In the golden light, its polished surface seemed to catch fire, every gentle curve softly embossed with Carlo's name. With trembling fingers, he unlocked the top and glimpsed at the pale powder shift like moonlit sand in inside. He unfolded the letter once more and let his gaze linger on the familiar handwriting:

"Ben,
If you're reading this, then I'm already gone, and I hope this letter finds you in a moment of stillness, when the world feels a little less heavy. I've never been one for grand

speeches, but there are things I need you to know.

You were my benedizione—the blessing I never saw coming but can't imagine my life without. You gave me purpose when I felt adrift, and hope when the world seemed too cold. Watching you become the man you are now, despite everything, has been my greatest comfort.

Now that I am gone, bring me home. Let the sea and the wind cradle me one last time, back to the island that shaped me. And when your own path leads you away from here, carry this place in your heart, as I have carried you in mine.

Remember, you're never truly alone. I'm in every wave, every gust of wind, and every quiet moment you steal by the shore.

Live boldly, Ben. You've always had it in you.
With all my love,
Carlo"

Ben's throat tightened around those final words: *Live boldly.* A prospect he never dared entertaining. He closed his eyes against the sudden hint of tears, summoned his strength, and tilted the cylinder. A pale veil of ashes drifted out, shimmering in spirals of opalescent dust before catching the breeze and gliding toward the glittering sea. For a timeless moment, they hovered above the water, gleaming like fragments of a broken rainbow, then slowly drifted down into the foam, dissolving into the endless turning of the waves. He remained kneeling, eyes fixed on the spot where Carlo's ashes vanished, letting the ceaseless crash of surf and the hush of the wind fill his senses. At last, he rose, the now-empty cylinder cool and weightless in his palm, but his heart lifted by an unexpected buoyancy. He gathered his pack, cast one last look at the cove shining below, and turned back along the sunlit trail.

~

The gentle whir of the bicycle's gears receded to a soft murmur as Ben eased himself down

the winding coastal road, back to the hotel.
With every rotation of the pedals he felt the
months of dread within him loosen, as though
each turn peeled away another layer of worry,
he had carried like ballast in his chest. With
Carlo now gone, and Ben unable to hold onto
the inheritance of the escape room museum,
the months following his death had been a
quiet whirlwind—of letting go, of finding
someone to take over the legacy Carlo had so
lovingly built, and of closing the chapter with
one final, dignified goodbye. Between searching for a new place to live and taking on a new
job, Ben had barely paused to breathe. And yet
now, coasting along the wind-bitten road, he
felt, for the first time in a long while, a hint of
lightness. When he finally reached the last
bend, the hotel came into view. Dark iron balconies jutted defiantly over the churning sea,
its windows dark mirrors reflecting nothing
but the endless horizon, as though the structure itself were holding its breath. He slowed
to a stop on the gravel drive, gathering his
weight as he slipped one foot from the pedal.
His trainers thudded softly against the stones.
He leaned the bicycle against a low stone wall

and climbed the broad steps leading to the lobby. Inside, the long corridor lay empty; the muted carpet swallowed the soles of his shoes, and his footsteps echoed sharply off the plaster walls. At the far end, he found the room marked with his number. The latch gave a solitary click as he opened the door and slipped into the hushed room. After a pause, he pushed open the balcony door.

Outside, warm air carried the rhythmic hiss of waves smashing into hidden coves below. Foam-tipped rollers advanced and retreated in silent choreography, and a late breeze toyed with the hem of his shirt. He inhaled deeply, letting the tension loosen in his shoulders as he leaned on the wrought-iron railing, watching the restless sea. That was when he saw the figure on the balcony just below. A tall man, broad-shouldered and alone, stood beneath the warm glow of the sun. Drops of water clung to his mahogany hair like polished beads—he must have emerged from the shower moments before. He wore a loose white terrycloth robe, the belt tied carelessly, and one hand rubbed a towel through his locks while the other pressed a phone to his ear.

Ben watched as the man paced slowly along the narrow terrace, each measured step betraying the weight of his conversation. Though the man's voice drifted away on the wind, indistinct and muffled, the furrow of his brow and the rigid set of his jaw spoke volumes: this was no ordinary chat. Anguish clung to him like a second skin, and his broad frame seemed bowed beneath an invisible burden. For a moment, Ben felt an unexpected kinship swell in his chest—two strangers bound by silent sorrows, each seeking release in the same salt-scented air. He lingered, curiosity and empathy kindling in his veins. When at last the man's phone call ended, his shoulders sagged, and the device dropped with a soft thud onto a marble-topped side table. The man eased into a wicker chair that creaked under his weight and buried his face in his hands for a moment before gazing out at the horizon as if hoping the sea might carry his troubles away.

Ben did not move, watching the silent plea in that bowed posture, the way the man's knees splayed against the railing. Then he drew back into his room and closed the door gently. But the image stayed with him: the solitary figure draped in sorrow, staring into the vast expanse as though seeking an answer in the depths.

That night, Ben found himself enveloped in the crisp, cool sheets of his hotel bed, beneath a canopy of unfamiliar stars that twinkled with a distant promise, but sleep remained just out of reach. His mind was a restless sea, tossing and turning with the memory of the man in the white robe—a figure both spectral and sorrowful. The man's gestures were deliberate, pointing beyond the jagged cliffs where the sea whispered secrets to the night. There was something magnetic, almost intoxicating, about this enigmatic figure, a pull that stirred a deep curiosity and a sense of longing within Ben, leaving him to wonder about the depths of the man's story and what truths he carried just beneath the surface.

Dawn arrived as a flush of violet and rose, spilling across the jagged shore. After he brewed a small cup of coffee in the kitchenette, Ben ventured again onto his balcony.

Sharp morning light carved the rocks below into craggy relief; foam rolled in restless tongues against their edges, and gulls wheeled overhead, their cries echoing in the crisp air. He raised the steaming cup to his lips, then let his gaze drift downward to the terrace below. There, the man sat once more, now clad in a lightweight linen shirt so sheer it revealed the sculpted planes of his torso, and faded jeans that moulded to powerful thighs honed by years of exertion. Morning light traced every ridge of his collarbone, every slope of his shoulders, and the firm line of a jaw accented with dark stubble. He leaned forward, elbows braced on the balcony balustrade, and eyes fixed on a distant point beyond the horizon. A jolt ran through Ben's ribs at the sight—not only at the man's physical grace but at the silent weight he bore. He knew it would be absurd to call down, instead, he drew in the warmth of his coffee and let the two of them remain in quiet accord, two solitary souls leaning on different balconies yet sharing the same longing for answers carried on the wind and waves.

~

Ben moved almost ceremoniously through the hotel's great lobby. The ceiling soared overhead, crisscrossed by ancient wooden beams, and crowned with wrought-iron chandeliers whose many faux candles glowed like captive suns. Pools of honeyed light spilled down onto clusters of plush, velvet upholstered settees; each one arranged as though awaiting secret conversations. A hush of voices and distant footsteps drifted through the space, as though the lobby itself had settled into a thoughtful silence. He let himself pause beside a tall pillar, one hand resting lightly on its fluted surface, as if anchoring himself in the present, reminiscing the morning's slow wander through the old town, where the air had tasted of salt and history in equal measure. The town's alleys had curved and twisted like a labyrinth, framed by pastel-coloured houses whose wooden shutters snapped closed in the breeze.

Between their walls, laundry lines draped across the sky, the sun, had tinted the spaces in a warm glow, with the air tinged with citrus from the lemon trees climbing the balconies above.

That morning, his journey led him to the wide piazza at the heart of the Wednesday market. He felt a connection to Carlo, walking the same paths and breathing the same air. He imagined Carlo strolling leisurely through the piazza amidst the bustling merchants. He could hear the lively haggling as vendors called out their goods. Baskets overflowed with fruit so vividly coloured they seemed almost unreal—clusters of tomatoes as red as polished garnets, apricots the colour of late summer sunsets, and lemons so pale and perfect that their rinds released a bright, nearly electric fragrance when touched. An elderly woman, bent with age but still exuding warmth, offered him a slice of fresh bread. Its crust cracked beneath his teeth like breaking winter ice, while the inside stayed soft and warm with steam.

He wondered if the old woman had known Carlo. He almost asked her but held back. Of course, they knew of Carlo—he thought, but Ben, like Carlo, was not ready to confront the broken legacy his name had left behind.

He was familiar with Carlo's descriptions of the island by heart. Ben did not want to face the shame and questions about "*lo sperduto*" —the lost one—as Carlo guessed they might have nicknamed him. Everyone on that island was known by a name derived from a memorable event in their life, a mishap they had experienced, or a parent they'd been born to. Names could identify someone precisely during the whispered gossip sessions between neighbours who peeked out of their door shutters without stepping outside. It was never a flattering nickname unless you came from a wealthy and respected family. If you did, you'd be known by your last name, and regardless of how many unrelated people shared the same surname, the naming system would unfailingly pinpoint the exact person. Thus, Ben wanted to avoid getting caught up in the addictive whirlwind of gossiping locals by not asking about Carlo.

Beyond the stalls lay the harbour, where fishing boats bobbed gently on the turquoise water, each hull painted in bold swathes of cobalt, scarlet, and jade. The nets were coiled in great loops on deck, pale as moons fallen to rest, and the fishermen—weather-bronzed men with stoic faces—moved among them with a practiced ease born of decades spent at sea. Above it all, seagulls wheeled and cried, their voices carried off on the wind to mingle with the distant church bells and the echo of children's laughter from the quay.

Now, back in the hushed sanctuary of the lobby, Ben's reverie was stirred by the sight of a low mahogany table near the reception desk. Its polished surface was cluttered with glossy brochures and dog-eared leaflets advertising different adventures: boat cruises to hidden coves, guided walks along nature trails, excursions along the old city walls. The brochures were printed in vivid colours—emerald greens, sapphire blues, and sunset oranges—all whispering of places waiting to be discovered. Ben reached forward, fingertips brushing the edge of a pamphlet titled "Island Walking Trails," and paused to read its sun-faded map. At that moment, another presence joined his own. A hand brushed his, slight but insistent, shifting the pamphlet by an inch. Startled, Ben lifted his gaze to find a man standing beside him—a figure half in shadow, half in the sun's glow, as though he had stepped out of a painting. Up close, he was more striking still: dark curls, damp at the nape, curled against a tanned neck; high cheekbones and a firm jaw carved his face into angular relief. His eyes were storm grey, deep, and restless, holding a flicker of something unspoken—perhaps regret, perhaps sorrow. He wore a linen shirt in soft white, the sleeves rolled casually to his elbows, and his posture was erect but not rigid, as though he carried heavy thoughts with quiet resolve.

"Sorry," the man murmured, his voice low and resonant, as he gently withdrew his hand. Their fingers had touched for a heartbeat— enough to send a warm spark racing up Ben's arm. "I didn't mean to—" Ben's pulse hammered in his ears, and he forced himself to smile. He sounded steadier than he felt. "No, really, it's fine. Go ahead." His words floated in the hush of the lobby, and for a moment they stood in stillness, the brochures forgotten.

The man's gaze drifted to the pamphlet in Ben's hand. "I was just... looking for something to do around here," he said after a breath. "I haven't done much exploring yet." Ben's smile widened, genuine now. "That makes two of us. This island is beautiful, though. There's so much to do!"

A half-smile touched the stranger's lips, but it didn't quite soften the tension in his eyes. "Yeah," he said softly. "I bet!" Silence fell once more, as thick, and luxurious as the rose-hued rug beneath their feet. Ben felt the lobby's grand proportions recede until it was just the two of them, suspended in a moment that felt both fragile and decisive.

Finally, Ben sensed an urge he could no longer contain. His cheeks warmed as he took a hesitant step forward. "I, uh... I noticed you from my balcony earlier," he blurted, words tumbling out with more urgency than he intended. The moment they left his lips, he felt raw and exposed. The man lifted an eyebrow, amusement flickering in the corner of his eyes. "Oh? I hope I wasn't putting on a show." Ben let out a short, nervous laugh, running a hand through his own hair. "No, nothing like that.

You just... looked like you had a lot on your mind."

The faint smile melted away, replaced by a softer gravity hidden by an awkward chuckle. "You could say that."

Ben swallowed, then extended a hand, determined. "I'm Ben."

The man studied him for a heartbeat, then took his hand in a firm, surprisingly warm grip. "Thomas," he replied.

Their handshake lingered a moment before they released, and as if by unspoken agreement, they fell into step together. The lobby's vast space reunited itself around them, the clink of cups in the café corner and the soft rustle of pages turning in the reading nook drifting back. Yet the distance between them had closed, and a gentle camaraderie hummed in the air. They walked side by side through the lobby doors and out into the late afternoon light. The hotel's white walls, warmed by the sinking sun, glowed with soft pink hues. Ben led the way along a narrow path lined with low stone walls draped in grey-green lichen, past clusters of lavender and rosemary whose oils rose on the heat in a comforting perfume.

When they reached the beach, the sand lay cool and pale underfoot where scattered shells and pebbles glinted in the last rays of daylight, and the horizon was a broad canvas streaked with coral and sapphire. The sea rose and fell in a steady breath, lapping gently at the shore. Thomas paused at the water's edge, shoulders drawing back and tightening as if bracing himself against some inner storm. Ben noticed the way his fists curled then relaxed at his sides— the subtle language of someone holding back more than he cared to reveal.

"Rough day?" Ben ventured softly, his voice low enough that only Thomas could hear. Thomas stood for a moment, eyes fixed on the shifting expanse of water, before he gave a slow, deliberate nod. "Something like that." They set off along the shoreline, leaving twin trails of footprints that the surf erased almost as soon as they appeared. Their words came sparingly, each one weighted with unforced intention, carried on the rhythm of the waves. Ben glanced at Thomas's profile: the line of his cheek lit by the dying light, the long sweep of dark lashes, the crease between his brows that hinted at sleepless nights.

Curiosity bloomed inside Ben's chest. "What brings you to the island?" he asked after a while, his tone gentle. Thomas paused mid-step, then allowed a small, rueful smile to form. "Work," he said, the single word sounding heavier than its brevity suggested. "I'm here for a medical conference."

Ben looked thoughtful. "So, you're a doctor, then?"

"Psychologist," Thomas corrected, with a quiet note of pride—or perhaps resignation—in his voice. His eyes drifted back to the water, as if searching its depths for something he had lost. Ben nodded slowly, imagining the weight of that profession. "I'm Ben, by the way," he added, though they had already exchanged names. It felt necessary to say it again, aloud, as if anchoring them both here.

"I know," Thomas replied, letting out another small chuckle. "I'm sorry—I just... you told me earlier." Ben offered a small, blushing smile attempting to hide his embarrassment. "I'm... a fishmonger," he said, staring down at the sand in the hope to change the topic. "I work at a little shop back in Scotland."

Thomas turned his head, eyes alight with

genuine surprise. "A fishmonger," he repeated. "That's... unexpected." Ben shrugged, lifting a foot to let the surf wash over it. "Not exactly glamorous. But it pays the bills. There's something honest about it—getting up early, selecting the catch, talking to people, and getting to know them." That last one was a lie.

Thomas studied him for a long moment as the sky deepened to indigo. "Life does take us in strange directions," he said quietly, steering Ben to surprise for such pivotal response.

They fell silent again, walking beneath a sky now freckled with first stars. The salt tang of the sea hung between them, and the horizon seemed to call out promises of hidden coves and unmapped reefs. In that soft twilight, Ben sensed that this chance meeting—two travellers brought together by a brush of fingertips and some unseen force—might be the beginning of something neither of them could yet name. And as the gentle surf swept over their footprints, he felt, for the first time that day, a stirring of anticipation for the path that lay ahead.

They strolled along the water's edge as the sun tilted west, splashing the sand in molten gold.

The breeze carried salt and the distant hum of beach chairs being folded up—a gentle hush that felt carved out just for them. In those quiet gaps between their footsteps and half-formed sentences, Ben felt an unspoken current coil around them, drawing their silences closer together.

Soon the crowds thinned, and they found themselves on a secluded curve of shore, where the only soundtrack was the steady drum of surf and the rattling of pine needles stirred by the wind. Here, time seemed to pause, the world slipping away until there was just this stretch of beach and the two of them. Thomas came to a halt and faced the horizon, where the sun's rim hovered on the brink of the sea. Ben slowed, watching the shrinking orb bathe Thomas in that dying light. Shadows carved along his cheekbones and down the line of his jaw, and the soft flare of pink on his collarbone made him look almost vulnerable. Ben's throat tightened. He wanted to close the space between them, to bridge whatever distance had settled into Thomas's posture.

"You seem...heavy," Ben said before he knew what he'd breathed out. Thomas blinked, as if waking. "Heavy?"

Ben gulped, suddenly aware of the words floating between them. "I'm not sure how else to say it. Your shoulders are hunched—like you're carrying something I can't see."

Thomas's gaze drifted back to the glowing horizon. He ran a hand through his hair, fingers coming away speckled with sand. The wind lifted loose strands, brushing them across his forehead. He exhaled, slow and low. "I guess I am." His voice cracked at the edges. "It's been a complicated few months." Ben waited, neither stepping closer nor pushing Thomas to speak. The hush of the waves filled the space, gentle and insistent.

After a long beat, Thomas turned his eyes on Ben. "I'm...in a relationship," he said, voice barely above the crash of water on sand. "Or I was. I'm not even sure anymore."

A twinge of something—jealousy, pity, surprise—fluttered through Ben's chest. He cleared his throat. "I'm sorry," he offered quietly.

Thomas shook his head, as if trying to shrug off the confession. "Don't be. I—I just dumped that on you." Ben lifted his chin. "No. I asked."

Thomas offered a faint smile, although the shadows lingered around his eyes. An unfamiliar sensation wrapped around him, almost paralyzing. This boy, this stranger, actually understood him. "Yeah, well, maybe I've been taking on too much," he said with a dry laugh. "More than I can manage."

That openness, honest and tremulous, struck a chord deep inside Ben. He understood what it meant to feel weighed down by your own secrets—how each one could press down on your chest until you could hardly breathe. In the fading glow, he reached out, thumb brushing Thomas's wrist as if to say, *I'm here.*

They walked on, side by side, the sky above bleeding pink and violet while the sun slipped wholly beneath the waves. They spoke in low murmurs; confessions and half-smiles weaving between the crash of surf and the cry of seabirds. The world beyond that strip of sand faded away until all that mattered was the two of them, sharing a moment that felt more intimate than either had expected.

As the sun sank ever more languidly toward the horizon, the sky shifted through a thousand gradations of colour: pale apricot bled into molten gold, which in turn deepened to burnished amber and finally bruised violet. Ben stood motionless on the sand, his skin raising gooseflesh along his forearms, feeling the world around him fading away until the only reality was the space between him and Thomas.

That gap shimmered with possibility—each heartbeat seemed to draw them closer, invisible threads tightening until their bodies were poised on the brink of contact. Ben's pulse thundered in his ears, drowning out the gentle hiss of the surf and the distant cry of a gull winging toward its roost. Every grain of sand beneath his bare feet pressed up at him in quiet solidarity, while the sea exhaled in soft, rhythmic waves. All his senses attuned to Thomas: the faint rustle of his shirt, the warm exhalation of his breath, even the muted creak of his jeans as he shifted his weight.

Thomas's dark eyes met his. They were luminous pools alive with something dark and profound. In that gaze lay the promise of wonder, of nights that might stretch on forever, of discoveries to be written upon their bodies and souls. Ben swallowed against the tightness in his throat, scarcely daring to inhale more than a fraction at a time, fearful of breaking the spell.

Time slowed to a heartbeat's echo. The wind stilled, and the rolling tide hesitated before its next advance. Then, as if surrendering to an unseen invitation, Thomas raised his hand to meet Ben's in a rushed and decisive gesture, though the contact felt lighter than breath, a feathered tracing that set Ben's nerves ablaze. He felt it as a current, bright, and sharp, zig-zagging beneath his skin. An involuntary gasp slipped from his lips, a sound so intimate it might have been stolen from his own chest. That single touch ignited a flame within Ben, like a spark to dry kindling. He turned to face Thomas completely, feeling the warmth emanating from his chest and the firm strength of his arms. The sharp line of Thomas's jaw caught the fading golden light, confident and defined. In that charged silence, desire blossomed into something rich and intoxicating, like a hidden garden unveiling its blossoms at dusk. Ben's legs felt both light and unsteady as he closed the small gap between them, their breaths mingling in the salty air. Was this a dream? Was it real? Just hours ago, this man was a stranger on a balcony, and now he was gently touching Ben's arm. Should he stop him? Should he act? Ben found himself both frozen and melting at the same time.

When their mouths met, it was as though two stars collided—brilliant, scorching, impossible to hold back. Thomas's lips were soon insistent and warm, the rough caress of his stubble against Ben's skin sending shudders rippling through him. Ben responded with equal urgency, hands weaving into the fabric of Thomas's shirt, seeking the taut planes of muscle beneath. His fingers pressed and explored, memorizing the living sculpture of Thomas's torso: the gentle flare of his ribs, the steady throb of a pulse under his palm.

Around them, the world dissolved: the tide's soft woosh retreated to a distant rhythm, the breeze became a mere caress across their heated skin. All that remained was the press of bodies, the slick slide of mouths on mouths, tongues darting and tasting, discovering. Each movement was both fierce and intimate, a silent confession that needed no words.

Gently, almost hesitantly, Thomas guided Ben

backward, away from the lapping tide, until the dry sand met their feet. It gave way in soft mounds, cradling their limbs as they toppled down together. The world tipped, then righted itself around their joint gravity. Thomas's weight fell against Ben's chest in the most delicious way—anchoring him, steadying him, making him feel cherished and seen. Ben's hands roamed upward to Thomas's neck and shoulders, fingers tracing the fine hairs at the nape, eliciting a low, satisfied sigh.

Thomas's arms curled around Ben's back, drawing him deeper into the swirling vortex of sensation. The curve of Thomas's hip pressed into Ben's. Their kisses grew softer, more searching; lips brushed across jawlines, along cheeks, trailing down to the hollow of the throat where every sigh and shiver felt magnified. The scent of Thomas's skin—warm, faintly sweet—wrapped around Ben like a spell, drawing him further under.

Above them, the first stars pricked open in the darkening sky. A lone shooting star arced silently overhead, its fleeting flame mirrored in the heat between Ben and Thomas. They paused, forehead to forehead, breathing the same summer air, eyes shining with mutual wonder. Something unspoken passed between them: gratitude for this unexpected moment, for the bravery it took to cross the chasm from longing to touch.

Then Thomas's hands slid beneath Ben's shirt, thumbs grazing over the tender skin at his sides, eliciting a gasp that was part surprise, part delight. Ben arching into the touch felt like an offering—and Thomas received it with reverence, as though every contour of Ben's body was a poem he ached to read. Their movements became a slow, sensuous dance, guided by breath and heartbeat rather than haste. A gentle tide of sensation washed over them, ebbing and flowing until the world seemed to narrow to this single point of perfect intimacy.

In a voice both husky and tender, Thomas softly whispered Ben's name, the sound barely audible, over the rhythmic crashing of the waves nearby. Ben responded with a breathy moan, a melodic note in the symphony of their shared movement, as their bodies entwined and shifted against the yielding sand beneath them. Each press and slide of their bodies was a silent vow, a promise forged in the salty air, the enveloping warmth, and their shared vulnerability. The cool night air brushed against their overheated skin, accentuating every contrast: the slick, glistening glow of sweat, the firm, unyielding press of muscle, and the intoxicating scent of two hearts beating in unison.

In a crescendo that was both fierce and gentle, they reached a shared release. Ben's cry echoed in the night; a sound raw yet exultant. Moments later, Thomas followed, his muscles relaxing around Ben in a gentle, tremulous embrace.

They lay entwined, wrapped around each other like vines, their breaths coming in ragged, uneven waves, their pulses racing as though they might be carried away on the currents of their shared experience. Beneath the velvet sky, moonlight draped them in silvered lace.

Thomas shifted, propping himself on one elbow to study Ben's face, a lazy smile curving his lips. His eyes—once fierce with desire—soothed into something warm and protective. Ben reached up, fingertips brushing a damp lock of hair from Thomas's forehead. His touch was feather-light, a recollection of the very first caress. "Are you okay?" Thomas's voice was a soft rumble, threaded with emotion and awe. Ben's heart clenched in silence with a warmth that went far deeper than physical heat. He nodded, pressing a kiss to Thomas's palm. "I've never been better." he whispered. Thomas's smile deepened, and he leaned down to capture Ben's lips again—this time in a gentle, lingering kiss that spoke of beginnings rather than endings. Beneath the tender press of their mouths lay a promise of mornings to come: dawns shared on this same stretch of sand, laughter carried on the wind, the slow unfolding of life's everyday wonders now tinged with the memory of tonight's blaze.

They lingered in the afterglow, limbs entwined, fingers tracing idle patterns on each other's skin. The night air cooled them, but neither minded; they had found within one another a flame that would burn long past the darkest hours. Above, the stars wheeled in silent procession, witnesses to a new world forged in heat and hush, in confessions spoken without words.

After a time, with the moon high and the tide's lull a soft murmur, Thomas offered his hand. Ben took it, and together they rose from the sand, brushing away fine grains that clung like glittering memories. Side by side, shoulders touching, they walked back toward the distant lights of the hotel. Their hands remained linked, hearts still echoing the night's wild symphony, each step carrying them toward everything they had yet to discover—together.

~

The next morning, Ben woke with the faintest tug of consciousness, as though someone were gently pulling him from a dream. Outside the windowpane, a chorus of sparrows and finches greeted the dawn in a delicate trill. Pale shafts of sunlight, hesitant and golden, slipped through the loosely woven linen curtains, painting the room in soft, honeyed stripes. They drifted slowly across the rumpled sheets, pooling at the foot of the bed, then sliding upward until the whole world inside glowed with quiet light. For a long moment, Ben lay beneath the billowy folds of pale blue fabric, toes curling against the cool mattress. He breathed in the lingering warmth of his shared body heat with the man now lying next to him—and in that hush, the events of the previous night drifted through his mind like a half-remembered reverie he longed to hold fast. He felt the steady thrum of his own heartbeat, measured and calm, but his thoughts flickered with the memory of every tender pause and whispered promise. Slowly, he turned onto his side and there, in the amber glow, he caught sight of Thomas. He lay curled beside him, shoulders rising and falling in a slow, deliberate rhythm—the same rhythm Ben had come to know as the pulse of this perfect morning. Dark lashes, thick and sweeping, cast faint shadows over high cheekbones. In that suspended moment, Ben understood. Here—in this room where their clothes draped carelessly over the chair by the dresser, where

leaflets and conference lanyards lay in a neat-
enough pile beside a scatter of coins; on the
nightstand, where a half-empty glass of water
stood untouched; here, by the open balcony
where Ben had first glimpsed Thomas from a
few floors above—was proof that it had not
been a dream.

He studied the soft curve of Thomas's neck,
where his rosy skin seemed to capture the
morning, adorned by a single lock of hair that
had slipped loose and fallen across his brow.
The tension that had furrowed Thomas's fea-
tures only yesterday was gone, replaced by
something infinitely softer, more vulnerable:
the man beneath a very carefully worn façade,
laid naked in the glow of a new day. A faint
smile played at the corners of Ben's lips as he
reached out, drawing the thin covers closer
around their shoulders. He nestled into
Thomas's side, heart fluttering at the warmth
of that small, perfect contact. In that stillness,
nothing beyond this bed, this moment, and
the soft susurrus of morning birdsong existed.
Ben and Thomas moved as if time itself had
paused for them. Inside that hotel room, the
world had ceased to exist. Thomas stirred, his

lashes fluttering like butterfly wings before parting in a slow, sleepy smile. With a languid stretch—limbs unfolding as gracefully as a cat's—he drew Ben close, their bodies entwined beneath the thin, sun-warmed sheets that had become their world.

By midmorning they slipped into the glowing lanes of the Sardinian town. Their footsteps led them pastel facades of tightly packed buildings, their shutters thrown wide to welcome the breeze. Shopkeepers sat in shaded doorways, gently sweeping early dust into the gutters, nodding greetings as the two passed. The air thrummed with the scent of *cascà* and warm focaccia, steam mingling with the ever-present brine of the open sea.

As the sun climbed toward noon, the pair arrived at the sprawling flea market in the cobbled square. The market buzzed with conversation and the clink of glass. Here Thomas sprang to life: his hands darted from one stall to the next, haggling over chipped ceramics and hand-blown glass vessels that caught the light like tiny prisms. Ben trailed a step behind, content simply to watch Thomas's face would glow each time he spotted some fascinating trinket, caught in an act of child-like awe.

They drifted among weathered stalls, pausing over hand-crafted linens, brass compasses with rusted hinges, and baskets brimming with citrus so golden it seemed to glow. Now and then, Thomas would brush Ben's arm—pointing out an old map or offering a taste of a perfumed fig. That soft, electric contact—fingertips grazing skin—sent Ben's pulse racing even amid the market's cheerful clamour.

Hours later, they made their way down to the water's edge, feet sinking into warm, ivory sand. The afternoon blurred into a stretch of time that felt both fleeting and infinite—a quiet journey of two souls drifting in and out of laughter, tangled in conversation, pausing now and then to see each other more clearly. Together they walked in companionable silence, the sun and surf speaking for them. Ben felt Thomas's hand slip into his, fingers entwining with a tenderness that needed no words.

When the sun began to dip, they settled at a tiny café perched on a bluff above the sea. Thomas lifted a glass of *Carignano del Sulcis* wine—its deep garnet colour catching the fading light, the scent of wild berries and sun-dried earth mingling with the salt on his breath—and rested his hand over Ben's. They simply sat in stillness, sharing the unspoken understanding that this perfect interlude was just that: a fleeting moment in a world too vast and uncertain to hold them indefinitely.

"It's my last night," Thomas murmured, his voice so low it risked being carried away on the whisper of surf. "I have to leave in the morning." Ben felt his throat constrict; words all tangled. He stared instead at the wistful glimmer of the wine, searching for defiance in its roseate depths. Ben's eyes, shadowed and soft, met his. "I—I don't want to," he admitted, and his voice broke like a wave upon the shore. Ben swallowed hard. Then, surprising himself with the rawness in his own tone, he whispered, "Then stay." Thomas shook his head ever so gently, a movement tinged with sorrow. "I know," he said, voice barely more than a breath. "But I can't."

That night, beneath the starlit rafters of their little room, no grand vows were uttered.

Instead, Thomas held Ben close, his chest warm and steady against Ben's ear. Fingers traced lazy, languid patterns along Ben's back, weaving promises half-forgotten, half-feared— promises that flickered between hope and despair. The night wrapped around them like a cocoon, and in its embrace, they surrendered to sleep.

When dawn broke again, the room was suffused with a soft, pale glow. Ben stirred, eyes fluttering open to find Thomas already at the window, lacing familiar, worn leather shoes. The hush between them was almost tangible, filled only by the distant cry of gulls drifting in on the air. Bent on one elbow, Ben watched as Thomas moved with careful deliberation— folding a shirt, smoothing its creases, packing a bag as though each small act might delay the moment of departure. At last, Thomas crossed the room and sat on the edge of the bed. His eyes—soft, storm-tossed—found Ben's. He reached up, brushing a stray lock of hair from Ben's forehead, then let his thumb rest against the soft curve of his cheek. "I don't want this to feel like a goodbye," he said, his voice thick with everything left unsaid. Ben closed his

eyes against the tenderness of that touch, the simple gesture anchoring him in the delicate present. "It isn't," he whispered, though his heart thudded with both longing and fear. Thomas managed a small, bittersweet smile. "I'll send you a sign," he promised. His thumb traced the line of Ben's jaw, each gentle stroke echoing with hope. "You'll know when."
With one last, lingering kiss—soft, urgent, laden with farewell—Thomas rose. He hauled his bag over his shoulder and paused at the doorway. For a heartbeat, the corridor beyond seemed to beckon him back inside, as if the walls themselves regretted his leaving. Then, quietly, the door clicked closed behind him.
Ben lay back against the pillows, that soft closure echoing in his chest like the final note of a song he wasn't ready to let end. It wasn't over—not yet. Somewhere out there, beyond the thin walls of this room, Thomas's promise waited to be fulfilled. And Ben, with hope newly kindled, would be listening—waiting for the first note of Thomas's sign to rise with the morning light.

5.

TIDE

"There is no greater agony than bearing an untold story inside you." —Maya Angelou

"For all the times I tried to say goodbye..." Thomas's words drifted into the cool, salt-thick air, each syllable lingering as if reluctant to disturb the hush of sunlight. He stood motionless on the jagged rock; the coarse stone pressing through the thin soles of his sandals and fought the urge to swallow the confession whole. His throat tightened, a coil of relief and dread pulsing with every heartbeat. Around him, a pale sea mist rose in slow spirals, pale tendrils that seemed to cradle his voice and carry it only as far as it dared. He drew in a long, trembling breath, balancing on the edge of a truth that might lift him or break him entirely.

The sun hovered on the horizon, its amber glow quivering across the gentle swell of the Baia d'Argento. Thomas's gaze never strayed from that golden path on the water, where light and shadow tangled like old regrets.

"...no one ever reached for me and pulled me back like Ben did." His whisper barely disturbed the tireless roll of the waves.

Gratitude and guilt warred in his chest—he owed that man everything, and yet the weight of his debt crushed him, despite a whole decade had passed. How cruel, he thought, that the one person who reached out his hand never stayed long enough to say a proper farewell. He closed his eyes against the memory of Ben's steady eyes, tasting salt and regret in the same stolen breath, certain the ache in his ribs would never loosen its hold.

The tide crept in, icy tendrils of water wrapping around his ankles, pulling with a persistence that mirrored the chaos inside him. A part of him longed to give in to that vast ocean—to step into the infinite blue and disappear beneath its waves. However, another part resisted, holding tight to the sharp refuge of rocks and memories. Oblivion called softly, while fear warned of losing himself completely in that water that mirrored the passage of time in the wrinkles on his face.

Memories surged like wind-driven waves, carrying him back to a childhood sheathed in polished façades and hushed mandates. He had grown up among a regimented row of white-stone villas in the Scottish suburbs—just miles apart, yet worlds apart from Ben— their walls gleaming ivory in the sun with lawns so geometric they seemed carpet of emerald blades precisely clipped they stood at rigid attention. Sculpted hedges arched overhead like silent sentinels, at the crest of the street loomed his family's house: broad marble terraces that reflected the late afternoon light, floors of veined Carrara stone that gleamed beneath the refracted prisms of crystal chandeliers. The faint, sweet tang of wax polish lingered in every hallway, proof that he belonged to something immaculate, untouchable. In the hush, admiration for his father's renown as a master surgeon glided on soft breath; his older brother's trophies caught the light through glass cases, their polished surfaces magnifying each accolade. Portraits of stern ancestors lined the endless corridors, their oil painted eyes daring him, with silent disdain, to falter. Childhood felt like a silent performance in those corridors, he learned early to become the consummate actor: grades so flawless they shone bright; laughter pitched high but never free; manners so graceful they seemed carved. His mother's gaze—bright, searching, an unblinking lantern—caught every tremor of imperfection. Even as a boy he deciphered the unvoiced tenets of their world: strength must be mute as marble, control unyielding as steel, vulnerability a blemish to be scrubbed from the surface.

A succession of claustrophobic dinners in the grand dining hall, where the scent of roasting herbs and sizzling fat curled through the candlelit air, where his small hands gripped the carved mahogany arms of the chair, knuckles whitening as his father, with surgeon's precision, carved perfect slices of roast beef under the soft clink of silver. Across the table, his brother—years his senior and already a prodigy—nodded along to their father's taut, precise remarks on anatomy and technique. Their conversation was a duet of scalpel-sharp intellect and muted pride. Thomas, too young to grasp the full weight of their exchange, mimicked their measured nods, offered clipped replies that closed doors rather than opened them. But in the rare, unguarded interludes, Thomas found a doorway to freedom. Just beyond the lichen-spotted stone walls of their estate lay a public park, its winding gravel paths and cathedral-like oaks seeming to exist in another realm. He would press his cheek to the cold iron bars of the gate, inhaling the green, loamy scent of dew-damp grass while watching other children tumbling across the turf, their laughter a wild, soaring chorus, their scuffed knees and grass-stained clothing proof of unrestrained freedom. He felt more foreign in those moments than anywhere else—an exile watching strangers perform rites he would never join. He envied their messy, unfiltered joy.

Medical school dawned over him like a blinding sunrise—inevitable, prescribed, dazzling in its precision. He donned the white coat and mask of conformity, burying every rebellious spark beneath layers of sterilization and protocol. At his white-coat ceremony his mother grasped his shoulders with trembling fingers, her eyes glistening like wet porcelain. "You'll make us proud, darling," she whispered into his collar, her voice so frail he felt it might shatter. The expectation settled on his shoulders like a shroud of lead.

Pockets of rebellion glimmered in those relentless days—most vividly at the pool, playing water polo under harsh fluorescent lights. When the referee's whistle blew, Thomas slipped into the water's cool quiet. Beneath the surface each stroke carved through chlorine-dulled blue, his limbs moving in precise conversation with the current. Here he was pure motion—powerful, unjudged, free. Breaking the surface, he'd gasp for air and lock eyes on teammates—bronzed bodies slicing through water, veins pulsing under taut skin. In the chaos of a match they collided, limbs tangling, trunks slipping down muscular thighs as hands clawed at hips or gripped nylon briefs in frantic bids for dominance. The water magnified every flexing muscle, every ripple of abs and calves kicking off the pool's tiles. Back in the locker room, the post-match buzz turned into a different ritual—a messy bond of sweat, chlorine, and swagger. The air reeked of damp fabric and male musk. Steam curled around cracked white tiles as laughter echoed off hard walls, punctuated by wet feet slapping concrete. Towels snapped across dripping backs; clothes vanished, sending teammates chasing each other naked through the locker room. Chest bumps landed with hollow thuds; back-slaps bloomed handprints on damp shoulders—primal, wordless affirmations of brotherhood. He'd found himself watching more than was necessary: a bicep flexed under a wrung-out towel, water tracing six pack ridges, thighs coiling with muscle. Once, a big guy shook off the spray like a wild beast, droplets flying, chest heaving. The sight stirred a nameless pull Thomas quickly buried, refocusing on his laces or the cracked tiles to distract his thoughts. The memory alone felt dangerous, a half-forgotten temptation pulling at threads he'd worked so hard to bind. He buried those stirrings deep, tucking conflict behind courteous nods.

All pretence unravelled the day he met Ben. In Ben's calm, unwavering gaze, Thomas glimpsed a doorway out of the script he'd been born to follow—and felt the terror of losing the single soul who saw him beyond his façade. He wasn't sure if he possessed the courage to step across that threshold, to voice the truths he had practiced to silence.

And so here he remained, all those years later, perched on this solitary crag by the hotel where they first met, the dying light and rising tide his only witnesses, torn between the safety of his unspoken past and the perilous promise of what might come next.

~

The first time Thomas caught sight of Ben, it was only a flicker at the edge of his vision—just another stranger walking through the hotel lobby. The instant Ben's motionless silhouette brushed past his awareness, something lodged in Thomas's chest, tugging at him in ways he both welcomed and resented.

Ben moved with a silence that tested Thomas's pulse sending it skittering—an intensity so contained it felt dangerous. Thomas tried to scold himself: be rational, maintain distance. Instead, he found himself drawn to that very stillness, to the silent arrogance of it. He was used to wearing masks—smiling on cue, meeting every expectation—but Ben looked like someone who needed no disguise. The idea both terrified and thrilled him. Falling—for once, Thomas wondered if he truly had fallen—happened with the speed of a snapped tether. One moment he was dutiful, secure in his rehearsed life; the next he was stumbling after a stranger's ghost of calm, heart hammering with desire and dread. There was no dramatic confession—only a brush of hands, a collision of impulse and doubt, as if he were tumbling into open air without a net.

They found themselves walking side by side beneath the glaring white walls of the Baia d'Argento hotel. Its grandeur pricked at Thomas's skin like needles. Yet beside the muted crash of the waves, all that formality felt far away.

Then their eyes met.

 Ben's gaze didn't judge; it simply absorbed, peering past the layers Thomas had spent a lifetime polishing. He saw the fear, but he offered no shock, no pity, just a steady calm that made Thomas ache with both relief and alarm. As Thomas walked along the shore, his mind was torn between two conflicting thoughts: one urging him to retreat to familiar safety, the other daring him to stay. He had always been the calm one, the reliable figure others turned to for reassurance—the quality Charlotte often praised as her support when her own worries threatened to overwhelm her. He had embraced this role, wearing it like a second skin. But now, as Ben's shadow stretched alongside his, Thomas sensed a crack in that carefully built front. He observed Ben, noticing the wind tousling his dark hair and the easy confidence in his stride, and felt a slow, unsettling change within himself. For the first time, Thomas questioned if he had confused his need for stability with a strength others had simply projected onto him. Maybe it wasn't Charlotte who needed grounding, but him. Perhaps he had held onto her out of a deep need for control, to quiet the chaos he feared within himself.

Here, there was no audience, no expectations—just the raw, unfiltered moment, and the man beside him who seemed to offer a kind of freedom that was both exhilarating and frightening. To follow Ben felt like a betrayal, but to step back felt like losing himself again. His heart raced, the cool salt air filling his lungs as he stood on the brink of a choice he had never truly considered before: who he might be without the roles others had assigned to him.

They moved in near silence, footprints swallowed by shifting sand, the sea's rhythm filling the spaces between their unspoken thoughts. Then, as if the ocean itself forced the confession out of him, Thomas wanted to speak, but paused, throat tight, certain he would regret every syllable. But Ben remained still, and in that unwavering quiet, Thomas recognized the heart of his conflict: the terror of surrendering control, the yearning for something genuine, and the nagging fear that if he let go of his carefully crafted self, he might never be certain who he'd become.

Ben stood beside Thomas on the wide, wind-swept beach. A chill breeze tugged at Ben's clothes, but he held his ground, shoulders relaxed, arms at his sides. His eyes were steady, unblinking, fixed on Thomas with a calm intensity that filled the space between them without a single word. The hush of the sea, the distant cry of gulls, the shuffle of grains of sand under their feet—none of it distracted Ben. It was as if he alone had been given the gift of perfect stillness, and Thomas, trembling, sensed that here at last was someone who simply wanted to hear him. Thomas shifted his weight.

When Ben finally spoke—his voice low and even, but warm—he simply said, "You seem...heavy," Those words landed against Thomas's ribs like a lifeline. His throat constricted; he swallowed hard. He whispered in admission tasting foreign on his tongue. He paused, held the silence in his chest for a moment as though assessing it for safety. The old fear came flickering back—fear of judgment, of disappointment. He dared not hope for kindness. But it was kindness he found.

"It's... complicated," he managed, his words

slow, deliberate. He glanced down at the tide pool forming a lace of foam at his feet, then looked back up at Ben's impassive face. He realized he no longer felt the urge to be polite, to put on a brave mask. A sudden urgency seized him: he had to speak, to let the dam inside him give way. His heart thudded in his chest, each beat echoing like a call to confession. He drew in a breath as if to steady himself, and then the words began to pour out in a ragged torrent. "I'm... in a relationship. Or maybe I was." The name that came next felt like a shard of glass in his mouth. "Charlotte." Saying it made his lungs shrink—guilt and longing twisted together in his chest like a double helix. A raw sting opened beneath his ribs, and for a moment he stared out at the water, memorizing the restless curve of each wave. He went back to that first moment when expectations had begun to close in on him. He was six years old, clutching a gold star certificate in a classroom lit by neon lights. His mother stood beside him, her smile as bright as the star itself—so bright, it felt like a promise he'd never asked for. He could feel his mother's hand on his shoulder, as if she were fastening him in place under the spotlight of that day, binding him from the very start to the pact of excellence they'd silently made the moment he was born. From then on, each new honour was another brick added to a tower built from other people's ambitions. He became the boy who sat at the front row, spine straight, shoes polished, hand always raised with the correct answer. He didn't miss school, didn't slip in his grades, never settled for second place or a passing mark.

Even as he excelled, that performance began to consume him from the inside.

He told Ben how every *well done* from a mentor felt like tightening a noose, how the applause at his white coat ceremony sounded less like celebration and more like the crack of a whip. He tasted bile as he stood on that stage, the weight of his family's pride settling on his shoulders like lead. His father's handshake was firm, his mother's whispered "You'll make us proud, darling" brushing against his ear with a rehearsed intimacy. Beside him, Charlotte beamed, her hand resting gently on his arm, the same approving smile extended to her as if she, too, were part of the family's triumph. In that moment, they must have looked like the perfect pair—an image of success his parents had always envisioned. Introducing Charlotte had felt like ticking another box in his family's unspoken checklist. With his older brother already married and expecting his first child, the news of his relationship with Charlotte seemed to complete the family picture, a final touch in their carefully curated façade of perfection.

"She's... been part of my life for so long," he said, voice low, as if the word might shatter if he spoke it too loudly. He let himself be carried back to earlier days: Charlotte's laughter echoing down deserted hallways, her bright eyes alight with plans for the future, her hand warm in his when they walked to their dorms from class. But just as vividly, he recalled the hush that settled over their evenings, the silent dinners as family members looked on with expectant smiles, the way she'd press her palm to his chest as if to say *We have to make this work,* as though love were something you could will into being by sheer force of will. In those moments, her eyes grew pleading rather than joyful, and he realized love had become another obligation—one more brick in his ever-climbing wall.

"I don't even know who I am without her," he said, voice barely more than a breath. His hands dropped to his sides, fingers splaying against the cool sea air. He dared not look at Ben, fearing he'd see shock or pity in those unblinking eyes. But when he finally met that gaze again, he found only quiet, unshakeable understanding. No pity. No surprise. Something deeper—a recognition that Thomas's chains were not unique, but had been worn by Ben himself, Carlo, and many others long before him. A nervous laugh escaped him, thin and brittle, like a crack in porcelain. "I've been carrying so much," he admitted, trying to sound casual, but each syllable trembled. He lifted one hand and ran it through his hair, tangling his fingers in damp strands. "We were never in love," he said, the truth cutting the air between them into shards. "It was easier, safer. Our families—both of them—wanted the same thing. Two ambitious kids who'd keep the legacy going. It was expectations, not feelings."

He turned away from Ben and faced the

restless sea, the salt spray stinging his face. His heartbeat pulsating in his ears. "She's everything they wanted for me," he said, barely louder than a whisper. Especially everything: the straight-A grades, the perfect manners, the future spelled out in neat, capital letters. "But she... she smothers me. Being with her feels like drowning. I... I can't breathe."

Now, standing on the taupe sands of the Caletta beach, that same yearning surged inside him—an urgent, breathless need to break free, to hurl himself into the churning sea and let the currents carry him into the silence of the underwater.

Ben's expression never faltered. He leaned forward slightly, as if drawn in by an invisible thread.

Thomas felt the quiet swell between them, the charged air pulling at his thoughts, as if the entire world had contracted to the thin ribbon of space between his trembling chest and Ben's steady presence. His heart pounded, and then, before he could stop himself, the darkest thought he had tried to suppress slipped free, tumbling into the open like a rock kicked loose from a cliff edge.

"I want her gone," he blurted, the words jagged and raw, their sharp edges cutting through the air. The syllables felt alien on his tongue, as though they had escaped before his mind could catch them, before he could mould them into something safer, more acceptable.

He looked at Ben and realised, with a jolt, that it was the first time in years he had spoken without fear. But then the shame hit him like a wave, cold and suffocating, surging up from his gut to his throat. His knees buckled, his stomach clenched, and his hands shook so violently that he clasped them together, knuckles going bone white as though he might physically wrestle the confession back into his chest.

"I—I didn't mean to say that," he stammered, the words scraping against his raw throat. His vision swam, the world tilting as though the very ground beneath him had shifted. He took a shaky step back, eyes darting to Ben's face, searching for shock, for judgment, for anything that might mirror the self-loathing flooding his veins. But the horror he expected never came.

Instead, he felt Ben's steady, unblinking gaze

on him, an unspoken reassurance that cut through his panic like a lifeline. Thomas reached out towards Ben without a word. *Please don't tell her anything*—he wanted to say, as if Ben could tell Charlotte about any of that. His fingers warm and reassuring as they closed around Thomas's trembling hand. The contact was electric and grounding all at once, a message without language: *I understand how you feel*. Thomas's panic receded by degrees; each gasp of breath felt a little easier. His pulse slowed, the tight knot in his stomach loosening as Ben's steady grip reminded him, he wasn't alone. He locked his gaze to Ben's face. No shock registered there, no judgment— only a gentle, unwavering acceptance that sent a curious thrill through him. The world paused. The gulls overhead stopped their cries. Even the restless ocean seemed to abide this moment of suspended calm.

Then something that had been smouldering beneath the surface finally flared into life: the fierce, forbidden pull between them. Lines Thomas had drawn in his mind wavered and fell away all at once. Without thinking, he closed the distance. Heart pounding with equal parts desire and dread, he reached for Ben's other hand. Ben leaned in, meeting him halfway.

Their first kiss was as though the world itself might shatter if they were too forceful. Lips brushed, a feather-light touch that set off sparks in Thomas's veins, igniting every nerve ending. He felt guilt burn like acid in his stomach, but even that guilt was laced with an intoxicating rush of relief. As their mouths met again, firmer, everything else—expectations, obligations, the weight of every well-meaning brick stacked by family and society—slid away. All that remained was the fierce, trembling hope of something wholly his own. He surrendered to the moment, heart hammering, pulse racing, breath coming in short, sweet bursts. In that lingering kiss, he tasted freedom and fear in equal measure, and for the first time in a lifetime, he felt entirely, achingly alive.

~

"I'll send you a sign," Thomas whispered, voice trembling like a live wire amid the roar of the restless sea breeze. He froze in the doorway, every muscle taut with longing, every nerve scorched by the memory of those two days together. He ached to turn back, to bury himself in the heat of Ben's body, to lose himself in that fierce, trembling heartbeat they had shared. But he stood still, fingers curled around the doorframe as though it were the final lifeline to the world they'd built here—just the two of them, suspended from time. On the rumpled white sheet, Ben lay bare and luminous, his skin slick with the imprint of their passion. The linens trembled with their heat; the air was thick with the ache of memories that pressed on Thomas's chest. With one last scorching look, he tore himself away and stepped into the corridor, leaving behind the man who had reshaped his world.

Weeks slipped past, but the island refused to release him. Its memories burrowed into his mind, gnawing at him in waking hours, haunting his dreams, lodging in his chest like a relentless ember. And Ben refused to go, his presence a phantom scent that trailed Thomas through every crowded street of their shared seaside town.

The absurd coincidence of it all—meeting someone from his own city, miles away abroad—clung to him with the same quiet persistence. What were the odds? That fate, or some cruel joke, had waited until foreign shores to tangle their lives together.

Thomas carried his business card in his pocket like a secret oath—a heavy weight of desire and dread. He fingered its smooth edges day and night, unable to force himself to Ben's door. Fear writhed in his gut: fear of breaking what fragile thread they'd spun on the island, fear that Ben had maybe moved on, that their union was nothing more than a fever dream. Yet the promise—his promise—pulled him forward until he found himself standing in the hushed stillness before Ben's front door, heart hammering so loud he was sure Ben could hear it from inside.

His mind flickered back to that sun-drenched afternoon. They had walked side by side along the narrow, crumbling cliff path, they had spoken of many things that day—of childhood fears, of broken families, of long-buried regrets—but it was Thomas's whispered confession that had hung between them like the blade of a knife, poised to sever the fragile thread of their connection. He had let it slip, a dark, desperate thought that had clung to the corners of his mind for months, festering like a wound. *I want her gone,* he had said, the words had tumbled from his lips before he could catch them, instantly feeling the cold wash of regret. But Ben had met his gaze with a quiet understanding. He had not flinched, had not pulled away, had not balked at the dark, forbidden thought that had slipped unbidden from Thomas's lips. He had simply absorbed it, accepted it, allowed it to slip into the unspoken fabric of their bond without judgment, without fear. And in that moment, Thomas had felt the first, faint flicker of something darker and more dangerous than desire—a fierce, unshakable loyalty forged in the slow, simmering heat of shared secrets and unspoken oaths.

He stood on the threshold, breath catching, every part of him screaming to push that door open, to fall into Ben's arms and drown in the storm of love that had consumed them. But he steadied himself, knowing this moment demanded sacrifice. With hands that shook like autumn leaves, he retrieved the card: *Dr. Thomas Davenport, Counselling Psychologist*, etched in precise black ink. This was the sign he'd vowed to send—proof that their story wasn't over.

Thomas pressed the card through the letterbox, the thin rustle echoing in the empty house inside, then stepped back. His pulse thundered for an eternity as he pictured Ben's fingers finding the card, Ben's eyes widening as he realized: this was their lifeline back to each other.

Days stretched on. Thomas threw himself into his practice, but the anticipation gnawed at him like acid. Every client blurred into the next until, one morning, his own appointment book yanked him from the haze. There it was: *Ben (New Appointment)*. Just few words, clinical and cold on the digital page, but for Thomas they roared with promise. His chest flooded with heat; his hands trembled as he tapped the screen, committing to the dangerous gravity of what was coming.

That day, he sat in his office at Hayfield Health Centre, the chill of the room pressing in on him. The tick of the wall clock was a drumbeat in his veins, each second dragging him closer to the moment he would see Ben again. Sweat glistened at his temples, his pulse a war drum in his ears.

Then the door opened.

Ben stepped in, and the air exploded around them. The electric current of their first meeting struck again—burning, consuming, inevitable. They greeted each other with practiced calm—patient and doctor in muted professional tones—but beneath the facade, the storm raged. Every stolen glance crackled with desire; every measured word carried the weight of their secret.

In those early days, they had perfected the charade, a whispered rebellion against the clinical walls of the health centre. When the corridor outside echoed with the sharp clack of heels or the muted murmur of passing nurses, they played their roles to perfection. Thomas would settle into his leather chair, one leg crossed over the other, his expression carefully neutral, his voice a polished, professional murmur as he inquired after Ben's "progress." Ben, for his part, would lower himself into the stiff, plastic-backed chair opposite, his head bowed, his fingers worrying at the frayed edge of his jacket cuff as though the weight of his imagined troubles had driven him to the edge of despair. They spoke of anxiety, of sleepless nights, of the shadows that clung to Ben's thoughts like sea mist to the jagged rocks of the bay. But beneath the surface, another current flowed—an understanding neither had to voice aloud, forged under moonlight and sealed in silence. It was a careful dance, a tightrope walk of whispered confessions and half-smiles under the threat of unsolicited visits from Dr. Charlotte Petersen.

The sessions were never just therapy—not really. They were a shield, a room wrapped in clinical oath of confidentiality, a sanctioned pocket of time no one could question. It was the only place they could meet freely, without eyes watching or questions trailing behind. Here, behind the safety of soundproofed walls and professional distance, they built a language of implication. They talked of burden, of breaking points. Of things "we carry" and people "we can't escape." Words of redemption and freedom circled the room like smoke, never quite naming what they meant—but meaning it all the same. And beneath them, a current of understanding: a plan unfolding between pauses and glances. Every pause between sentences held a second rhythm, a memory from that night on the beach—when Thomas had whispered the unthinkable, and Ben had not flinched. They had made a silent promise then, tangled between surf and stars, hearts still swollen with the delirium of new closeness: something had to change. The sessions gave them the time to shape that promise into something real. A plan. A sequence. An escape.

But when the hallway outside fell silent, when the muffled footsteps faded into the distance and the faint hum of fluorescent lights was all that remained, the masks slipped. Thomas would lean forward, his eyes darkening with the unspoken promise of the life they dreamed of, his fingers curling around the armrests of his chair as though bracing himself against the force of his own longing. Ben's pulse would quicken, his breath shallow, his gaze darting to the thin, frosted glass pane in the door that offered only the barest illusion of privacy.

It was in those stolen moments, when the antiseptic cold of the health centre seemed to tighten around them like a noose, that the dam broke. Thomas would rise from his chair in a single, fluid motion, his hand reaching for the lock with practiced ease, his breath coming in short, ragged bursts as he turned to face Ben. Their eyes would meet—dark, burning, unguarded—and in that instant, the thin veneer of professionalism shattered like glass. Their mouths would collide, a fevered union, and every touch was a match struck in dry tinder. Hands tore at clothing. Bodies pressed together. The sterile walls vanished. Breathless urgency eclipsed thought as skin met skin in frantic, searching movements. They would stumble backward, their limbs tangling, their breaths mingling in gasps and whispered promises as they clawed at the fabric that separated their skin. They moved with a frantic, unspoken understanding, each touch a silent vow, each kiss a defiance against the grey, suffocating walls that had tried to contain them.

And when the footsteps returned, echoing down the hall with the steady, relentless cadence of the life they had rejected, they would pull apart, their breaths mingling in the air, their hands trembling with the force of their shared desire. Thomas would adjust his collar, his fingers smoothing the rumpled fabric of his shirt, his eyes darting to the thin, frosted glass of the door as he forced his breathing to slow. Ben would settle back into his chair, his chest heaving, his pulse still racing, his eyes never leaving Thomas's face as they waited for the footsteps to pass, for the world to fall once again silent, for the charade to resume. In that moment, the room, the ticking clock, the title of doctor and patient—all of it dissolved. There was only them, burning bright and hungry, writing the next chapter of their dangerous, beautiful story in each other's trembling limbs.

~

Beyond the rugged, dark basalt formations jutting from the shore, at what felt like the edge of the world, Thomas felt the unyielding passage of time pressing upon him, gently yet persistently reminding him that all journeys, no matter how far-reaching or challenging, inevitably circle back to their beginnings. For Thomas, his heart had always guided him back to this very beach—this place where everything had started with Ben.

They called him "*Lo Straniero*"—The Stranger, the outsider who appeared on the island all those years ago and never left. Despite the sun-kissed lines etching his face and the years of sunshine captured in his aging body, Thomas' eyes still sparkled with the light of that last sunset. His rugged good looks continued to catch the eye of the island's lonely women. He joined the locals in playing *boccette*, sang loudly in the local café during big matches, attended church services, and participated in town processions, even though he was never particularly religious. He worked alongside the locals, conversed with them, and seamlessly integrated into their tranquil, slower-paced lives, quickly becoming a familiar face on the island. He was accepted without question, having earned their trust. His nickname carried no malice; *lo straniero* was simply who he was—a stranger who had found a new home.

He closed his eyes and drew in a slow, measured breath, filling his lungs with the chill, saline air that tasted of ancient depths and whispered tumult. Beneath that rush of brine, he detected the faint, herbal sweetness of wild fennel sprouting from cracks in the cliff above him. In that solitary, inhaled moment, the breath of the sea calmed his racing heart: vast, unchanging, and eternal. In contrast, human lives flickered like tiny candles caught in an unforgiving storm—fragile and dazzling for a moment, then snuffed out without warning. His own life, Ben's, Charlotte's: each had burned bright and then faded into darkness. For decades he had laboured to marshal the chaos of memory into tidy compartments of guilt, grief, and yearning. He had arranged every recollection as if it were an exhibit in a museum—pain neatly displayed behind glass. But memory, like the restless sea, refused to remain orderly and motionless. It crashed and churned, shifting shape at every turn. Destiny and fate, those invisible strands weaving souls together, yielded to no human logic or plea. The only alternative, Thomas had reluctantly learned, was endurance—an endurance sustained by the fragile hope that at some distant horizon, the tangled skein of existence might finally unravel into meaning.

Death, he knew too well, was the inexorable anchor dragging all living things beneath the waves. Thomas had witnessed it many times—in quiet, merciful passages and in sudden, brutal tragedies—but none struck him so deeply as Ben's. It was that loss, abrupt and final, that had hollowed him out. In the space where warmth and promise once resided, there echoed only a chilling void.
They'd dreamed of a future together—a small stone cottage on the edge of a windswept moor, where Thomas would be waiting once Charlotte was no longer an obstacle, once Ben had joined him. In their sessions, they sketched out a life of slow mornings and dusky evenings. A wild garden would bloom with heather and foxgloves; the cool air tinged with

the crisp scent of pine and wet earth. On the weathered stone steps leading to the garden, Ben would roll up his sleeves, while Thomas dangled bare feet over the edge of a battered, moss-covered bench, their fingers laced as the wind whispered through the gorse bushes clinging to the hillside.

Afternoons would find them wandering through dense forests of ancient oaks and whispering pines, their branches creaking in the cool breeze from the nearby loch. They'd duck beneath the low-hanging boughs of twisted rowan trees, their hands brushing against rough, lichen-covered trunks, the damp, peaty earth clinging to their boots. They'd pick brambles from thorny bushes, their fingers stained purple, their laughter booming through the dappled light as they chased one another through the thick, rustling ferns. When evening fell, they'd retreat to their small stone hearth, the fire crackling and spitting as it consumed the twisted branches of fallen pine and ancient oak, the sharp scent of smoke mingling with the tang of wet wool and dried mud. They'd sip smoky whisky from thick, chipped glasses, their shoulders brushing as they whispered across the flickering firelight, the shadows stretching long against the rough, whitewashed walls.

They would speak of lochs where they'd wade together, slipping through the frigid water over smooth, algae-slick stones, their breath catching in their chests as the icy shock of the mountain spring enveloped them. They'd tumble into the heather-strewn grass by the water's edge, limbs entwined in the long, wind-bent shadows of the hills, their breaths mingling with the damp, mossy earth beneath them. And once more on the cottage steps, they'd toast with rough, unfiltered whisky, their hands sticky with the dark, tart juice of freshly picked blackberries, to the life they'd taken back from grey obligations, watching their hair silver in the same pale light that had once cast their shadows long and golden across the hills.

But instead, Thomas stood alone on the train platform, wind whipping his coat, dread pounding in his chest. He watched the train's whistle fade, windows streaking past in a blur of glass and steel, his breath misting the cold morning air as the world rushed on—leaving him stranded, forever waiting for a man who never came.

~

When Thomas opened his eyes again, he gazed at the horizon where sea met sky in a diffuse sweep of molten gold and blush. He felt, deep within the curl of each advancing wave and the hush of each retreating swell, the ancient weaving of their lives—threads spun by forces far older and more cryptic than any human heart. Long before their paths crossed on this wind-scoured shoreline, he sensed, the cosmos had conspired to interlace their fates beneath the same sun and stars.

Ben had been an elemental force: capricious as a tempest, compelling as the tides. Within his arms, Thomas had tasted a life unshackled by duty, tradition, or expectation. Yet Ben never permitted a farewell.

In the weeks that followed his death, Thomas

found himself sinking into a maelstrom of guilt so profound that he nearly lost all grip on reason. They had dreamed together of escape, but those hopes shattered the moment Ben leapt the tracks.

Now, as the rough, sun-warmed stone pressed against his aged skin, Thomas found his perspective slowly and subtly shifting. He began to ponder the intricacies of Ben's final act, questioning his initial belief that it was a rejection of love. Instead, he considered the possibility that it was an abdication, a surrender to a suffering too immense to bear. The darkness that Ben carried had always been a shadow Thomas saw only in fleeting glimpses, never fully understanding or experiencing its weight himself. As he sat there, with the rhythmic and eternal murmur of the sea around him, Thomas came to a profound realization. He understood that both he and Ben had been grappling with their own despairs, each reaching a critical breaking point they could no longer ignore. The realization struck him with the force of a revelation, as he acknowledged the depth of Ben's struggle and his own limitations in offering consolation. In that quiet moment of reflection, Thomas understood what he hadn't been ready to before—that their lives had always been tangled together by burdens too heavy for either of them to carry alone.

And somehow, within that realisation, a fragile peace began to take root. Ben, in his own quiet, devastating way, had fulfilled what Thomas could only now see as his purpose. He had shaken Thomas from the hollow life he'd been living—the weight of duty, the rehearsed version of himself he had worn for so long. And then, slipping beyond the edges of life he had always hovered near, Ben had done the only thing left. He had freed him. His story had ended, as certain and inevitable as the sun sinking behind the hills. And in its place, something unexpected remained—not only grief, but a quiet, aching kind of gratitude.

His thoughts drifted then to Carlo—the weathered sailor who had rescued Ben from obscurity after the flames claimed his childhood. Carlo had offered shelter where none existed, taught young Ben the stubborn art of resilience, and revealed the wild beauty that thrived in the windswept crags above the bay. Though

Thomas never met the man in person, Carlo's presence lingered in his soul—steady as a lighthouse guiding ships through darkness. He thought of Charlotte, slender and immaculate, her outward grace concealed a grief that no polite conversation could touch. The suicide of her brother had shattered her core, hollowing her out in ways that no exterior perfection could mend. From that moment on, she clung to an ideal she could never fully own. In trying to preserve the flawless image, she had drained Thomas of the very vitality Ben had rekindled. In truth, Thomas realized, Charlotte had died the night her brother did— her spirit consumed in an irreparable void. The body found later in the museum's subterranean wing had only freed her from a life already lost.

He sighed, letting the bracing air sweep through his chest and clear away the last vestiges of agitation. For the first time in years, he felt the tension loosen; the compulsive need to force order upon chaos could finally yield. He could simply be present, a solitary figure at the water's edge. Thomas felt the moment approaching ever since he had emerged from the final swim of the day, clad in nothing but that tight, damp speedo clinging to his skin. Every rock beneath his feet felt like a milestone marking the long, winding path he had followed to arrive here. The sea, faithful as ever, lapped gently around his ankles as though urging him to step forward.

"I only wanted to make things right," he murmured to the wind, his voice disappearing into the ceaseless susurration of waves.

He turned at last to see the Carabinieri officer towering over him. The young man's uniform was crisp, his cap perched precisely, his eyes earnest. There was no weapon in sight—only a leather notebook clasped in one hand and an air of compassionate resolve throughout his resigned confession. He drew near and laid a firm but gentle hand on Thomas's shoulder.

"Signor Davenport," he said in quiet, respectful tones. "It is time."

Thomas inhaled one last measure of the sweet, briny air and let it out in a slow, deliberate exhale. The sun had dipped almost to the horizon, a molten orb casting the bay in liquid gold. The windows of the Baia d'Argento glowed like thousands of tiny lanterns in memory of the afternoon when he and Ben had stolen their first kiss by the beach's edge. He nodded, allowing the officer to help him to his feet. The cool water slipped over his ankles, sending a final, shuddering pulse through him. He had known they would come—ever since the fateful rose had washed ashore.

~

The morning the desert rose washed ashore, the tide had drawn back with an uneasy hush, leaving behind the usual detritus—seaweed, driftwood, tangled fishing lines. But nestled among them, half-buried in the Ravenscraig sand, was something unusual: a jagged, flower-like mineral, its twisted gypsum petals clinging to a stone like the curled fingers of a drowning man.

Isla McNab, a retired geography teacher out

walking her dog, noticed it first. Her terrier had darted toward the object, sniffing curiously before recoiling. Intrigued, Isla bent down, brushing away the kelp. At first glance, it looked like a fossilized rose—weathered, salt-crusted, but oddly pristine in its symmetry. She turned it over in her gloved hands, there, deep in the folds, something dark marbled the mineral: a rust-red stain, stubborn and strange. It was the peculiar shape that tugged at her memory. Years ago, she'd read about an artifact gone missing from a local museum—the only object unaccounted for the night a young woman had died there. The article had shown a photo, grainy but unmistakable: a desert rose. That was enough to make her bring it to the police.

The desk sergeant blinked at the crumbling thing before fetching his reading glasses, drawn in by the haunting shape. A report was filed. The mineral was tagged. And for weeks, it sat in the evidence room, catching the sterile light like the blade of a half-drawn knife.

Lab tests took time. But when results finally returned, they carried weight like a dropped gavel. The dark residue wasn't just iron oxide or sea algae—it was human blood. Trapped deep in the mineral's sheltered folds, shielded from salt and sunlight, the traces had clung stubbornly to the fossil despite its years beneath the sea. Analysis revealed two DNA profiles, partially degraded but clear enough for a match.

Dr. Charlotte Petersen. Her DNA clung to the fossil's jagged edges like a desperate grasp.

But it was the partial fingerprint, faint but shockingly intact, embedded in a concave fold of the stone, that sent a chill through the lab.

Angus MacRae.

Ben.

It was enough to reopen everything.

Charlotte's death was no longer an accidental fall through the forgotten shaft in the museum's under croft—it was a murder. The desert rose had been the one item missing from the crime scene—presumed lost or stolen in the chaos. Its sudden reappearance was more than coincidence.

With the fossil's return, the puzzle assembled itself with devastating speed.

Ben's disappearance. The bloodied ballast at the tracks. Charlotte's solitary wandering that night. Thomas's conspicuous absence from their shared home. And then, the private sessions—dozens of them—where Ben and Thomas had whispered about escape routes, parallel lives, the invisible seams between right and wrong.

Thomas remembered every step. How he had led Charlotte through the quiet museum, pretending to marvel at relics while his thoughts pulsed elsewhere. How he had stepped outside simulating a phone call he had to tend to, lighting his first cigarette in years, heart clanging with guilt and anticipation. How Ben had promised to take care of the rest.

The fossil proved he had.

But Ben never came.

At dawn, the train screamed through a red-drenched silence. A body lay beneath its path. The future they had sketched in stolen glances vanished like smoke.

Thomas had stood at Charlotte's funeral, a study in quiet grief. People thought he mourned his partner. They didn't know his sorrow was for the man who never boarded the train.

~

Now, as the officer recorded each of his admissions in neat, deliberate script, Thomas felt an unexpected lightness blossom in his chest. The years of secrecy, self-imposed exile, and unbearable remorse were unravelling like an old rope left to fray at the edges. When the metal cuffs clicked shut around his wrists, he did not flinch. There was no will left to fight—only the calm of resignation.

He turned for a final look at the bay. The dying light set each cresting wave aglow, as if the water itself had been transmuted into molten metal. Behind him, the hotel's stone façade glimmered softly, as though offering a last *benedizione.*

The officer guided him toward the waiting car. When the door closed, the hush of brine and breeze was sealed away. And in that silent, tender suspension between what was and what must come, Thomas carried with him the ultimate, unutterable truth: that freedom and fate, birth and death, delight and despair were

all cast upon the same shifting currents—and
at last, his own story would find its final shore.

A Note from the Author

This is not a story I wanted to write; this is a story I had to write.

For All the Times I Tried to Say Goodbye began as a quiet attempt at self-redemption—a way to lay my past to rest, to process the tangled web of memories and emotions that life has woven into my mind. What started as a series of disconnected scenes and fleeting thoughts from long-forgotten corners of my imagination slowly grew into a full narrative, a story that demanded to be written, no matter how painful or challenging the process.

I wrote this book over the course of two years, weaving my own experiences into the lives of fictional characters, each of them carrying a piece of my history, my fears, and my hopes. Ben, Carlo, Charlotte, and Thomas each represent a fragment of my past, a reflection of the person I was at various stages of my life, and the person I have fought to become. In a way, this book is my attempt to close those chapters, to assign my damage to characters who can carry their weight for me.

Writing this story has been a deeply personal journey, often exhausting but ultimately cathartic. It has forced me to confront the darkness that lingers at the edges of memory, to find meaning in the shadows, and to accept that some doors must be closed for others to open.
Every word, every scene, every line of dialogue has been a step toward understanding myself a little better, toward finding peace with the parts of me I once struggled to accept.

I am not a professional writer, nor do I aspire to ever be one. I wrote this book not for fame or fortune, but for the quiet satisfaction of holding my past in my hands, bound in ink and paper, and setting it free.

If you have read this far, thank you.
Thank you for taking a chance on a debut author with a story born of solitude and introspection. If these characters spoke to you, if their struggles resonated even a little, then I have succeeded in my humble mission.

About the Author

Lorenzo di Bernardo is a British-Italian writer, former seafarer, and civil servant currently living in Kirkcaldy, Scotland. His journey to storytelling is as complex as the characters he creates, shaped by years spent at sea, the quiet resilience of small coastal towns, and the introspective solitude of a life in constant motion.

Before settling in Scotland, Lorenzo worked on tankers and cruise ships, navigating the world's oceans and witnessing the raw, untamed beauty of the open sea—a perspective that often informs his writing. He later transitioned to a career in the civil service, where his sharp analytical mind found new purpose, balancing the chaos of modern life with the quiet introspection that writing demands.

Lorenzo holds a BSc(Hons) in Combined STEM from The Open University and an MSc in Applied Data Analytics from UHI.
For All the Times I Tried to Say Goodbye is his debut novel, born from a deeply personal need to confront the past, assign his traumas

to fictional characters, and find meaning in the darker corners of the human mind. The book blends the atmospheric, windswept landscapes of Scotland with the sun-bleached shores of his hometown Carloforte, reflecting Lorenzo's own life divided between two worlds.

When not writing, Lorenzo enjoys reading, exploring the Scottish countryside, and spending time with his beloved tuxedo cat, Teo.

Acknowledgments

I would like to extend my gratitude to the people who helped this manuscript reach its final stage: Daniele, Nick, Irene, Mel and the unwavering support of friends and family who believed in this project – the final steps to publication would not have been possible without you.
To my parents, who loved in the ways they knew how—for what was given, and what was meant.
A special thanks to Amazon KDP for enabling publishing for indie authors like me that otherwise would not be able to express their voices.
A thanks to *Ben, Thomas, Charlotte,* and *Carlo* for taking over my burdens and making them their own.

And to all those who doubted, dismissed, or tried to break me—thank you. You made me sharper, louder, and impossible to ignore.
You made me an author.